WINTERKILL

WINTERKILL

A NOVEL BY

MARSHA FORCHUK SKRYPUCH

SCHOLASTIC INC.

Copyright © 2022 by Marsha Forchuk Skrypuch

Photos ©: 279, 280: Courtesy of the author; 282–283: Jim McMahon/Mapman®.

All rights reserved. Published by Scholastic Inc., *Publishers since 1920*. SCHOLASTIC and associated logos are trademarks and/or registered trademarks of Scholastic Inc.

The publisher does not have any control over and does not assume any responsibility for author or third-party websites or their content.

No part of this publication may be reproduced, stored in a retrieval system, or transmitted in any form or by any means, electronic, mechanical, photocopying, recording, or otherwise, without written permission of the publisher. For information regarding permission, write to Scholastic Inc., Attention: Permissions Department, 557 Broadway, New York, NY 10012.

While inspired by real events and historical characters, this is a work of fiction and does not claim to be historically accurate or portray factual events or relationships. Please keep in mind that references to actual persons, living or dead, business establishments, events, or locales may not be factually accurate, but rather fictionalized by the author.

Library of Congress Cataloging-in-Publication Data available

ISBN 978-1-338-83141-2

10 9 8 7 6 5 4 3 2 1   22 23 24 25 26

Printed in the U.S.A.   40

First printing September 2022

Book design by Maeve Norton

TO THE MEMORY OF RHEA
CLYMAN, WHO WAS FIERCE IN
HER PURSUIT OF TRUTH

CHAPTER ONE
THE SHOCK BRIGADE

February 1930, in Felivka, a village near Kharkiv, Soviet Ukraine

Tato and I had just entered the village after inspecting our wheat field. There we stood, father and son, in front of Saint Sophia Church in silence and watched as hundreds of uniformed young people armed with leaflets marched past us.

A lot of them looked to be in their early twenties, and they wore the distinctive uniform of the Komsomol—the Young Communist League—beneath their unbuttoned winter coats: brownish-gray short pants gathered at the knee and a military tunic topped off with a red neck scarf and a belt across the chest. Their tall black boots made an intimidating thump as their feet hit our muddy road in unison.

There were also Young Pioneers, with their red ties visible above their coats. Young Pioneers could be as young as nine and as old as fifteen, but most in this group looked to be about my age, twelve. I was a Pioneer on paper because you got into trouble if you didn't join, but around here people called the red tie "the devil's noose."

There were also some adult marchers in city clothes, as well as others in the uniforms of youth leaders.

It took a while for them all to pass by. We waited another minute or so, then Tato and I stepped onto the road and followed them.

The Saturday market was in progress in the square, and as the strangers marched past them, our friends and neighbors stopped mid-haggle and gawked at the parade just like we had done. The marchers continued north up the street, and we continued to follow. Tato and I didn't have much choice, because our house was as far north as you could go and still be within the village.

Once the parade got past the village square, the marchers dispersed. I noticed a couple of them approaching Pani Pich's cottage, while three stood at Comrade Olinyk's door.

By the time we got to our own house, the parade had dissolved. I pushed open our door, grateful to be away from all the drama.

"Son, husband," said Mama, her face frozen in an artificial grin. She was seated at the table with my nine-year-old brother, Slavko, and eleven-year-old sister, Yulia. My chair and Tato's were occupied by two strangers. "We have company, all the way from Canada."

A Young Pioneer girl wearing her red devil's noose

around her neck sat at my spot beside Yulia as if it were hers. She had been scribbling something on a form when we walked in. The other visitor was a man sitting beside Slavko, in Tato's spot. He wore the kind of collared shirt with buttons that Roman, the priest's son, sometimes wore when he got a package from relatives in America.

The sight of them occupying not just our house but our places at the table sent a wave of fury through me. It was bad enough that Stalin had become the dictator of all the republics in the Soviet Union, but now he was starting up his "five-year-plan." It was supposed to modernize the Soviet Union but actually hurt people like us. He was taking away our farms and making them into one big collective farm—the kolkhoz. He had already sent in city people ignorant of farming to force the change on us, but now he was sending in foreigners. They couldn't possibly know the challenges we had. Every single day since Stalin's push had begun last year, friends and neighbors had been bullied and forced into giving up their property and joining the kolkhoz. But why Canadians?

"Slavko, go to Auntie and Uncle's barn and feed the animals," said Mama.

I was extremely jealous as my brother excused himself and ran out the door.

"Sit," said Mama, giving Tato and me each a look that said, *Don't argue.*

I had a barn to repair and chores to do, not to mention homework, but I was supposed to sit and be nice to these Canadians as they told me how to live. I pasted a smile onto my face. I'd be polite until we could get them to leave.

The man smiled. "Comrade Chorny, Comrade Nyl." He spoke perfect Ukrainian but with an odd accent. "I'm Comrade White. I go by George White, although my Ukrainian name was Yury Bialek. Let me introduce you to my daughter."

The girl looked up and smiled. "I'm Comrade Alice."

Tato sat in Slavko's spot. I pulled up an extra chair and sat down across from Alice and Yulia. "You came all the way from Canada to assist with Stalin's five-year plan?" I asked.

"We did," said Alice. "A new tractor factory is being built in Kharkiv, and once it's finished, my father will work there. In the meantime, we're helping with the drive to get people signed up for the kolkhozes."

Her Ukrainian was almost as smooth as her father's, but the accent was more pronounced. With her light brown hair and hazel eyes, she could have been a local, but the blouse and skirt had that fine weave and careful stitching that you only saw in clothing that came in packages from North America. It made no sense that they had come here. Living in America was the ultimate dream, yet they left it to come back here to help Stalin?

"What's that written on your pin?" asked Yulia, staring at the ornament on the Canadian girl's lapel.

Alice unclipped her pin and handed it to Yulia. "It's in English script, but the words are the same as on the Young Pioneer pins here. It says *Always Ready.*"

"I have one too," Yulia said. She scrambled from her seat and came back with her pin in her hand and her red tie draped loosely around her neck. She set her pin on the table so we could see the Russian beside the English. They had the identical image: Lenin with a Soviet star and flame in the background. I smiled and pretended to be interested in the whole show. I had a pin as well, but I never wore it or my devil's noose.

"Was there a Communist revolution in Canada?" I asked.

Comrade White cleared his throat. Mama gave me a look.

Yulia gazed longingly at the Lenin pin from Canada.

"Do you know what we should do?" Alice asked Yulia.

"What?" asked Yulia.

Alice slid her pin in front of Yulia's spot at the table. "Let's trade pins."

Yulia's eyes went wide. "Oh my," she said. "Do you mean it?"

"I do," said Alice. "Here."

I watched as Alice expertly tied the devil's noose around my sister's neck, then fastened the pin to the left side of her blouse. Yulia looked like she was about to burst with pride, and I had a sick feeling in the pit of my stomach. My sister seemed far too impressed with this girl from Canada.

"Don't you look smart," said Alice as she straightened my sister's tie. "Now promise me you'll take good care of your new pin."

"Of course I will," said Yulia. "And I hope you'll enjoy wearing your Russian one."

"I will," said Alice.

While this whole exchange was going on, I looked across the table at the paper Alice had been filling out. Even reading it upside down I could see that it was a checklist of household items written in Russian. The sections listing our pots and pans and dishes and clothing were already filled out. She'd made a special note of our hand mill for grinding hard grain and our loaf pans too. This was alarming.

Tato had sat down beside me in Slavko's chair. Mama served mugs of mint tea even though it was time for lunch and my stomach was grumbling. I think she was hoping the visitors would leave; two extra mouths would use up a lot of our food. Unfortunately, both father and daughter looked settled in and comfortable. Comrade White launched into a speech to Tato about the advantages of living on a kolkhoz while the rest of us stayed politely silent.

As her father talked, the Canadian girl looked around at the icons on our walls and frowned. Her attitude was typical of all the pushy shock workers—those Russians sent from Moscow, like Comrades Tupolev and Chort—and the locals who had bought into their lies, like Fedir's father, Comrade Berkovich; my old teacher, Comrade Holodnaya; and that stupid Comrade Smert. Alice also glanced at the glass bowl of decades-old pysanky—colorful hand-decorated eggs—that graced our table and at Mama's delicate embroideries covering the windows, but she seemed to be blind to their beauty. She just counted each item on her fingers, then noted the quantity on her form. She kept on glancing over to the corner of the room where Mama prayed. It was simple but functional, just a small table covered with a white embroidered cloth. There were beeswax candles on either side of an intricately carved crucifix.

Alice leaned over the table and said, "That's going to get your family into a lot of trouble." She pointed at the prayer corner. "You really should get rid of it."

"My great-grandfather carved that crucifix," I told her. "It means a lot to Mama."

"Then hide it," said Alice.

"We made atheist's corners at school last week," said Yulia.

"You should replace it. I'm serious," Alice said.

Mama held her finger to her lips. Alice sighed and continued with her inventory. Comrade White sounded like Tupolev, the head shock worker, in his arguments about why we should join the kolkhoz. "You'll get tractors and modern equipment for farming. We'll work together, and everyone's quality of life will be better. We'll grow more grain than ever before."

"Have you ever been a farmer?" asked Tato.

"No. I'm a tractor machinist," said Comrade White.

"That's impressive," said Tato. "I would never dream to advise you on making tractors, so why are you advising me on the best way to farm?"

"There's no reason to be rude," said Comrade White. "Don't you understand that I'm trying to help you?"

"Don't you understand what the revolution was all about?" asked Tato. "We got rid of the landlords and became our own bosses. Now Stalin wants to give us new landlords and take away our land."

"You realize that your words are treason, don't you?" said Comrade White. "The only farmers who insist on owning land are the kulaks, and they're the enemies of the revolution."

I felt like I had a stone in my stomach. Being labeled a kulak was serious. The term used to simply mean a rich farmer, but now it was applied to any farmer that the Stalinists wanted to eliminate. If Comrade White denounced Tato as a kulak, we could be executed or sent to a slave labor camp in Siberia.

Tato took a deep breath, then slowly let it out. I could see it in his face that he regretted his outburst. He didn't respond right away but then finally said, "I'm sorry. I spoke out of turn."

The uncomfortable silence was broken when Alice set down her pencil and said, "Who would like to help with the inventory of the outside?"

"I would," said Yulia, a bit too eagerly.

Mama's eyes landed on me. "Nyl," she said. "You can help Alice with the inventory."

"But I want to," said Yulia, her eyes filling with tears.

"You, young lady, need to feed the chickens and do your homework," said Mama.

I knew what Mama was doing. The chickens would be happy with their early meal, but Mama wanted to keep Yulia away from Alice. Yulia was far too eager to hear what Alice had to say.

"Yes, Mama," I said, getting up from the table. "Comrade Alice, I would be happy to help you."

I tried my best to keep the rage out of my voice. There was only one reason for Alice to be doing an inventory and that was so she could report to Tupolev all that we owned. It would help him know what he could steal. I wished more than anything that we had a way out of this situation, but I feared we did not.

Alice stood up, and I walked to the door. She followed, but she didn't look happy about going with me instead of my more congenial sister.

"You speak English and Ukrainian?" I asked her as we walked out the door and around to the back. I was determined to sound friendly. "How come?"

"I've spoken Ukrainian and English since I was little," she said. "I'm picking up Russian now, since everyone in the Communist Party seems to prefer it."

"I know what you mean," I said. "We understand Russian—there's a lot of similarities with Ukrainian—but we prefer to speak our own language."

"Me too," she said. "Russian feels funny on my tongue."

"That's our storage shed," I said, pointing to the wooden structure with a sod roof beside the barn-in-progress. Between where we stood and the storage shed there was a large mound of composting manure. As it rotted, it made good rich soil for our family vegetable garden, but it also had another purpose: It sat on top of a stone-lined storage cellar where we had hidden our precious store of millet, corn, and wheat seed as well as emergency sacks of wheat for eating. The trapdoor to the cellar was undetectable unless you knew exactly where to look. We walked right past it as I led Alice to the storage shed.

I opened the door for Alice, and she stepped inside. The shelves were lined with glass jars filled with preserves made from our own garden: pickled beets, cucumbers, and carrots. A brine barrel of cabbageheads sat in one corner, while hanging down from the ceiling were onions, garlic, and various herbs. There were also a couple of small burlap sacks of wild dried mushrooms and larger sacks of potatoes.

"No flour or grain?" Alice asked.

"The government requisitioned all of it last fall," I said. "In addition to our entire harvest, they took our stored wheat."

"You do have some wheat," she said. "I noticed the hand mill and loaf pans in the kitchen area."

"This is what we've been living on," I said, pointing to the items in the storage shed.

"No grain at all?" she asked.

"Just enough for our family to get by until the next harvest," I said.

It was almost the truth.

"Can you show me where it is?" she asked, holding up her inventory sheet. "I'd like to take note of it."

"You probably already tallied it," I lied. "It was the sack in the kitchen pantry."

"What's this?" she asked, stepping in front of our barn-in-progress. The outside structure was nearly finished, and I was still in the midst of putting up barn board partitions inside for individual stalls. Half of our barn was for animals, and the other half was to store sacks of grain.

"Our barn burned down in the fall," I told her. "We're building a new one."

"Where's your livestock?" she asked. "I'll need to inventory that as well."

I took her across the road. "That is my aunt and uncle's house," I said, pointing at the big thatch-roof cottage with a clay exterior tinted a cheerful yellow. "They're letting us use part of their barn for our animals until our new barn is finished."

"What's their last name?" she asked, flipping through her papers. "Is it Chorny, like yours?"

"Yes," I said. "Why?"

"Papa and I are supposed to do the inventory on that farm later today."

I led her around the back, and we stepped inside the barn together. Our animals and Auntie and Uncle's were in separate sections, so I led Alice to our area. While I breathed in the familiar musky smell of our dear animals, Alice wrinkled her nose and a momentary look of disgust passed over her face.

Manka, our cow, stood munching hay in the closest stall. She raised her head briefly to look at Alice, then me, with her liquid brown eyes. She seemed neither startled by nor interested in the stranger. She lowered her head and took another mouthful of hay.

I stepped forward and gently lay my head on Manka's cheek. "What a good girl you are," I cooed under my breath as I caressed her flank. The cow pretended to ignore me but I knew she liked this sort of attention.

"Would you like to say hello to her?" I asked.

Alice stood there, looking uncomfortable. She put her inventory list under her arm, then gave the cow a limp wave with her hand. "Hello, cow," she said.

"Not like that." I guided her closer to Manka. "Put your face on her cheek."

Alice stepped back. "I don't think so," she said. "That cow really smells."

"This is what cows smell like," I said. "If you lived on a farm, you'd find it pleasant."

"I don't live on a farm," said Alice. "And it's not pleasant."

"Manka's with calf," I said.

"She's pregnant?" she asked, her eyebrows raised.

"She is," I said. "She'll give birth in April."

Alice stepped in and peered at Manka's stomach, then quickly stepped back.

"Do you want to scratch her between the ears?" I asked.

She shook her head.

"I've got something else to show you." I guided her around the corner to the next stall.

We came up to our new mother ewe, whose fluffy white head came nearly up to my shoulders. I squatted a bit so I was at eye level with her, then scratched her head between the ears. She leaned into me so I could scratch her head more thoroughly.

"Oh," said Alice. "What a cute sheep. Does she have a name?"

"This is Fluffy, and she's a ewe, not a sheep," I said. "I know, Fluffy's not a very original name. Would you like to scratch her head?"

Alice smiled, then looked from my face to Fluffy's. "Will she bite me if I do that?"

"Hold your hand out to her first," I said. "She'll want to smell you. Then squat so you're at eye level with her. She'll feel less intimidated if you're not towering over her."

"Like this?" asked Alice, squatting low.

"That's perfect," I said. "Now you can scratch her between the ears."

Just then, Slavko rounded the corner, Fluffy's lamb, Bebe, cradled in his arms.

"What an adorable baby."

Alice reached out to pat the lamb's head, but I grabbed her hand to stop her. "Slavko's the only one who Fluffy trusts to look after Bebe."

"Oh," said Alice. "I wouldn't have thought an animal would be so particular."

"They're like humans, with their own personalities," I told her. "They're not tractors."

She frowned at that, and I wished I could have taken back the comment. I didn't want her to think I was making fun of her, even if I was. We stepped back a little bit to give Slavko room. He set Bebe down underneath Fluffy, then held a finger to his lips to ensure we'd stay quiet. Bebe sniffed around a little bit, found one of its mother's udders, and began to nurse.

"Let's give them some quiet," I whispered. I guided Alice out of the barn, and once we were well clear of it, I said, "Bebe only recently started to nurse. For the first few days, Slavko fed Bebe with a bottle and rag."

"What a smart boy," said Alice. "How old is he?"

"Nine," I said.

"What an asset to the kolkhoz he'll be," she said.

I stopped myself from saying something rude. I wanted her to like us so she wouldn't report us as a kulak family. Also, I was determined to show her what our life was really like and why you couldn't just box it up and turn it into a factory. In the long run I knew it wouldn't do any good. After all, it wasn't like she was in charge, but I still wanted her to understand why we loved our way of life. "Do you want to see our pasture area?" I asked.

Alice seemed more relaxed now. "I would."

We walked back across the road to the pasture behind the barn-in-progress. Yulia was now there, sitting on a tree stump doing homework. She'd let the chickens out and they were squawking and pecking around her. Yulia looked up and sighed as we walked by, then went back to her work.

"Look at this view," I said to Alice, pointing east. You could see all the way down to the wide river that bordered our village, and the fruit and willow trees that grew close to the water. "Soon those fruit trees will be covered with pink and white blossoms and the willows will be silvery green."

I noticed her studying our windmill atop a small hill overlooking the river. "With the heavy grain requisitions, that's not used much anymore," I said. "But before that, on days with a good wind, people from all over our village lined up to get their grain ground into flour."

"Who owns the windmill?" asked Alice.

"We do," I said.

"I suppose you charged people when they used it," said Alice.

"We ground the flour for them," I said. "We kept it clean and in good repair. Why wouldn't we charge a fee?"

"That's capitalist," said Alice.

"Machinists like your father get paid, bakers get paid. Why shouldn't we get paid to mill flour?" I asked.

"The mill should be owned by the community so people can do it themselves." She added notes to her inventory list.

"It doesn't matter anyway," I said. "The government took our grain. No one has anything to mill."

She looked over to me and scowled. "You know that's not true."

Her words made me squirm. I could have kicked myself for being so argumentative.

I looked around to see what might distract her and noticed Silney, our chocolate-brown mare, grazing at the other end of the pasture. I whistled, and she trotted over.

Alice looked up from her form and smiled. "What a beautiful horse," she said. "Can I pat her?"

"She might nip you," I said. "Give her a minute to get used to you." I caressed the side of Silney's neck. "Are you having a good day, my darling?" Silney shook her mane at me and snorted. "It's been that kind of day, has it?" I asked her. I kept on caressing the side of her neck.

Alice hesitantly held out her hand, and said, "Hi, Silney, my name is Alice."

Silney sniffed Alice's hand.

"Stand beside me and pat her here," I said, guiding Alice over to where I stood.

Alice reached up and caressed Silney's long neck, and Silney, to her credit, tolerated it.

"Silney is better than a tractor," I said. "She doesn't run out of gas or break down. Not only that, we love her."

"She is beautiful," said Alice.

"If we joined the kolkhoz, what would happen to Silney? What about the other horses?" I asked.

The question seemed to startle Alice. "I never thought about that," she said. "But surely they'd find a use for them."

"And who would care for Silney?" I asked. "She'd be common property. She'd lose the love we give her."

Alice's eyebrows puckered, and I hoped she was thinking about what I said. Our farm and our family were more than just cogs in a machine for producing grain. I stood in silence while Alice filled out the rest of her inventory, and I shuddered at the thought of all that I loved being reduced to items on a list.

Just then, there was a loud banging sound.

Alice looked up. "You're supposed to go to the village square," she said.

"More speeches?" I asked.

"Always more speeches," she said. "But also, something else."

CHAPTER TWO
VICHNAYA PAMYAT

Alice and her father stayed behind to finish the inventory while my family and I walked to the village square. Our next-door neighbors—Ruslana, Vera, and their father, Comrade Olinyk—joined us, as did other friends and neighbors. Villagers, activists, and shock workers all mixed in the square along with dozens of newly arrived soldiers who were decked out in full combat gear.

"Any idea what's going on?" Slavko asked, standing on the tips of his toes, trying to get a better view beyond the clusters of people around us.

"I can't see much either," I said, frustrated by the fact that I wasn't much taller than my younger brother. I was stronger though, so I crouched down. "Jump on my back."

He scrambled up, then shimmied up to my shoulders. "I've got a great view now. I can see the whole village square including the council building, the church, and the priest's house. I can see all the way to the kolkhoz construction site behind the square and the fields behind it."

"That's great," I said. "What's going on?"

"Fedir's father is carrying a chair," he said.

Comrade Berkovich set the chair down and jumped up onto it like it was a podium. "Comrades," he shouted in a booming voice. People stopped their chatting. "Look over there!" He pointed at the hill behind the kolkhoz construction site.

"It's a flag on a long pole, Nyl," reported Slavko.

At first, I saw nothing, but then it came into view. A hammer-and-sickle flag wobbled back and forth from atop a long flexible pole. Moments later, the top of a boxy shape appeared. As the thing crested the hill, its giant wheels were visible.

"It's a tractor!" shouted Slavko.

Sitting in the driver's seat was a young man in a Komsomol uniform. As he drove the tractor out of the field and onto the square, the villagers backed away from it to make room. The tractor ground to a halt. The engine shuddered, then stopped.

Slavko slid off my shoulders and nearly landed on Yulia, who was standing beside us. "I've got to go and see it," he said. He and Yulia both ran to get a better look, so I followed them.

Comrade Tupolev broke through the crowd and sprinted

over to the tractor. The driver stepped off, and Tupolev climbed up. Perching himself on the driver's seat, he looked down at us.

"The Soviet Union is the only country in the world that manufactures modern farm equipment like this tractor. Our modern equipment will make it possible to transform small farms into food factories. There will be more grain for everyone."

Slavko wormed his way forward, and before I knew it, he had his hands on the tractor with such gentleness and respect that you'd think he was scratching the ear of one of our farm animals. Next, Yulia was beside him and other kids crowded around too, fighting among one another to touch the tractor, to get a closer look. I stepped closer, but as I did, the crowd surged. Someone's hands pushed on my back, and I ended up right against the tractor. I grabbed onto it so I wouldn't get crushed.

And that's when I noticed a small metal crest with something written on it. It was affixed to the body of the machine at the back. The letters were not in Cyrillic, so it wasn't written in Ukrainian or Russian. The letters looked English, like on Alice's pin, or the packages Roman got from America. I didn't know what the letters meant.

Why would a tractor made in the Soviet Union have a label in English on it?

Comrade Tupolev continued with his speech. "No

other farmers in the world have tractors. Only Soviet farmers have tractors," he shouted.

My neck got hot with anger as I listened to his words. If he was going to lie to us, couldn't he at least make himself more convincing? Did he think that anyone in this crowd would believe a Soviet tractor would be labeled with English letters?

Why was he lying?

Tupolev paused to catch his breath. He looked around at his audience, then glared at two women who were whispering to each other. One of the women paled when she noticed his gaze. She elbowed her friend and they both fell silent.

Tupolev continued. "We have to watch out for traitors. Those who want to stop our progress. Selfish kulaks who only care for themselves." He paused again, then lifted his arms high in the air.

Suddenly, the church bells rang out.

Comrade Tupolev pointed to the church, and I turned to look. "Who is interrupting my speech by ringing church bells?" he roared. "We have saboteurs! Kulaks! Enemies of the people! We must fight them! Down with the church! Down with religion!"

Chaos broke loose all around. People from the city who one moment ago had been standing quietly, listening, unbuttoned their winter coats and took out banners, mallets, and nails. They ran through the village square and swiftly nailed the banners to every wall and post that they could find. The banners had slogans like *Down with the Church* and *Long Live the Kolkhozes*. Watching their orchestrated actions was like watching a play.

"Get the priest," shouted Tupolev. "He's behind all this."

A soldier ran to the priest's house and kicked down the door. Moments later, he came out, dragging Matushka, our priest's wife, by the black kerchief that usually covered her hair, only now it was around her neck like a noose. She gagged and choked with each step as he dragged her. "You're a traitor, a kulak," shouted the soldier. He drew his gun and shot her in the chest.

I stood and watched in frozen horror as blood blossomed on her chest and she went limp. The soldier strode back into the house. Another gunshot.

I wanted to do something. To help. But I just stood there.

The soldier came out, dragging the limp form of Father Ivan by the chain of the gold crucifix around his neck. Once our dear priest's body was beside his wife's, the soldier took the gold chain and crucifix from Father Ivan's neck and put it in his own pocket.

While the soldier was busy at the front, there was a flash of movement at the back of the priest's house. Roman, my classmate and friend—and now an orphan—had crawled out the back window. He was barefoot, and his black-framed glasses were crooked on his face. I looked around. The other shock workers had run off, and Roman wasn't in anyone's line of sight except my own. I did a quick motion with one hand, telling him to get going. He sprinted away from the house and hid behind a gravestone in the cemetery beyond the church.

"Tear down the church!" shouted Tupolev. "Now!"

I stood in outraged silence as soldiers, Young Pioneers, and other shock workers from the city rushed toward our church. Some used their mallets, while others took out rocks or bottles from their pockets. All of this was clearly pre-planned. They threw and smashed and screamed, breaking the antique windows and pulling off timber and stone. A man in a Komsomol uniform leaned a ladder up against the side of the church and a shock worker carrying ropes climbed onto the roof, then shimmied up the cupola and lassoed the cross on top. He threw the other end of the rope down to the ground, where other shock workers grabbed the rope and pulled. The cross toppled loose and fell to the ground. A woman from the city ran up to the front doors of the church, screeching at the top of her lungs. The doors were always left unlocked so people could pray when they wanted to, yet now it appeared that they were locked. The woman kicked and smashed at the doors with a hammer until she made a hole that was big enough for her to crawl through, then pushed the doors open from the inside. She propped one of them open with the ornate silver baptismal font, then went back in to do more damage. Moments later she emerged, wearing an altar cloth like a scarf and carrying the wooden icon of Saint Sophia and her three daughters, Faith, Hope, and Love. Our church was named after Saint Sophia, and this particular icon, with halos made with flecks of gold, was the most beloved of all. The woman lifted it above her head and threw it down the church steps. As the ancient wood split, I felt like my own heart was bursting. Next she threw off the altar cloth and stomped on it. As the woman went back inside, I stood there, frozen to my spot.

If I were brave, I would have tried to save our Matushka and Father Ivan. If I were brave, I would have gone to the church and tried to stop that woman from doing more damage.

But I was a coward.

Just then, the top part of the bell tower moved. I stepped back, not quite sure if I was hallucinating. All at once, the heavy brass bells came loose from the inside and smashed to the ground. The belfry toppled sideways off the tower and slid down the roof, then hit the ground and splintered into dozens of pieces. I thought of all the times those bells had beckoned villagers to come and pray. I thought of all the times Tato and I had been up there together, ringing them with joy and exhilaration.

Those bells were not just a source of joy though. The bells warned us of danger. What would warn us now?

It was like my feet were glued to the ground. I could not move. The priest and our church were the heart of Felivka. I had just stood and watched as our heart was ripped apart. When our church was nothing but rubble, the shock workers and activists left the square. Some of the ones who had been in the parade now headed out of the village toward the train depot, but the soldiers and the locals still milled about.

It seemed like hours had passed, but maybe it was only minutes because it was still daylight. A hand settled on my shoulder. I turned. My neighbor and classmate, Ruslana.

I looked around and realized that many friends and neighbors had gathered around the corpses of our Matushka and Father Ivan. Our classmate Oleh, his mother and grandfather, even Vanko, Sokolov's son. Auntie Pawlina was there too, her eyes wet with tears, but without Uncle Illya and without baby Tanya. I put my arm around her. Roman wasn't there. Hopefully, he was far away by now.

Just then, I saw Tato, clutching his staff with white-faced Mama by his side. Tato had been injured during the war, and his back was permanently damaged. He looked like he was in agony, and Mama looked like she was about to faint. When they stood beside me, Mama leaned heavily on me for support. Pani Holota appeared next, her hand steadying Comrade Olinyk, who was shaking like a leaf.

Ruslana ran over to help her father, then her sister, Vera, appeared. "We need to give Matushka and Father Ivan a respectful funeral," Vera said. "We need to carry them to the closest house and prepare their bodies."

Comrade Tupolev pushed his way through the crowd. "No funerals," he said. "That's just superstition. A cart will be around shortly to pick up the bodies. All of you, go home."

"We can't just leave them like this," I said.

"I don't think we have a choice," said Tato.

"Maybe we can't give them a proper funeral," said Mama. "But we must remember them." She grabbed my hand in one of hers and Tato's with the other. I reached for Ruslana's hand. We all joined hands and circled around Father Ivan and Matushka.

Vera breathed in deeply, then exhaled. She tipped her head to her sister, then in a clear solemn voice, she sang "Vichnaya Pamyat"—Eternal Memory. The ancient chant was sung for funerals and this felt like a funeral, not just for Father Ivan and Matushka but for our church, our bells, our community. Ruslana joined in, and the sound of the two sisters' strong sorrowful voices was like an acknowledgment of my own despair. Mama and Tato sang, and so did I. One by one, more voices chanted, mourning the destruction of our core, our place of worship, our place of joy. What made the violence even worse was that it wasn't an enemy doing it—it was Stalin—who was supposed to be the father of our country.

My classmate and friend, Fedir, stood in the distance. I motioned for him to join us, but he shook his head.

Just then Fedir's father pushed through our group. "Comrades," he said in a firm but low voice. "Please, break it up. You don't want to aggravate Tupolev."

"You should be ashamed of yourself," said Comrade Olinyk. "Betraying your neighbors the way that you've done."

Comrade Berkovich looked stricken by the comment. "No," he said. "I've been smoothing things over the best I can. The kolkhoz is coming, whether we like it or not."

"What's going on here?" Tupolev strode in among us, hands on hips and a stormy look on his face.

"They were just leaving," said Comrade Berkovich. He turned back to us. "Go home, everybody."

The crowd dispersed.

I had walked half a dozen steps beside my parents in silence when, suddenly, I realized that Slavko and Yulia weren't with us.

"I can't believe I don't know where they are," said Mama, looking panicked and pale.

Tato leaned on his staff, and it was like he had aged a decade in just this one day, but he was doing his best to help Mama. "We need to find them," he said. "What if they got trampled in all this upheaval?"

"Can you take Mama home?" I asked. "I think she needs to rest. And the kids may have gone back. I'll stay here and see if I can find them."

"Come, Mychalyna and Stefan," said Auntie Pawlina. "I'll walk home with you. Illya's probably frantic; I've been gone so long, and he's at home with the baby."

My parents shuffled down the street toward our house, and I was grateful that Auntie Pawlina was assisting them. They both looked so frail. The murder of our holy mother and father and the destruction of our church had sapped the lifeblood from them.

I pushed through the crowds, shouting, "Yulia! Slavko!"

No answer.

Panic overwhelmed me. How could I have left them like that? It was all my fault. My heart felt like it was about to jump out of my chest, and I could barely get enough breath. I forced myself to stand still and take deep slow breaths until my heart slowed down. It didn't quell the panic, but I was better able to think.

Where had I last seen them?

The tractor.

I pushed my way through the crowd to get there.

Slavko was crouched down by one of its giant wheels. "That's dangerous," I said, grabbing his arm and pulling him clear. "What if someone started it back up, or pushed it from behind? You could be run over."

"You should see it, Nyl," said Slavko. "This tractor is quite smart. I would love to make tractors when I grow up."

"I've been watching him," said Yulia, still wearing her devil's noose and the Canadian Lenin pin on her blouse. I hadn't noticed her standing off to one side.

"Thank goodness," I said. "You're both safe."

"Why wouldn't we be safe?" said Yulia. "We stayed right here the whole time."

"Why didn't you follow me?" I asked. "I had assumed you were right behind me."

"There was pushing and shouting," said Yulia. "In the crush of people, we lost sight of you. The only thing I knew to do was to stay exactly where we were until things settled down."

"Come on," I said. "We have to get back home. Mama and Tato are worried sick."

As we walked toward our house, we passed more of the city people who had arrived with the parade. They were all heading toward the train depot. Were Alice and Comrade White also leaving? It would be a relief if they were. At least then we'd be able to mourn in private.

But when we were nearly home, I heard a gunshot in the distance. A few moments later, we passed Comrade Chort, a nasty smile on his face and a pistol in his hand. The sight filled me with dread.

CHAPTER THREE
WILLOW CRADLE

Uncle Illya lay in the snow in front of their house, slick red blood covering his chest and staining the snow around him. Auntie Pawlina knelt beside him. "Sit up, Illya," she pleaded, tugging at his arm.

Mama and Tato stood off to the side, looking pale and still. Both leaned heavily on Tato's staff. Yulia and Slavko ran to them.

I approached my aunt and uncle and put my hand on Uncle Illya's neck. No pulse. "He's dead, Auntie." I wrapped my arms around her and tried to get her to her feet.

"The baby," she said. "Where is she?"

My heart went cold from fear. "Slavko," I called. "Come and help Auntie while I check inside."

Slavko ran over and propped up Auntie Pawlina while I ran into the house.

Dead silence. A mug of tea and a half-eaten slice of bread with cheese on the table. The willow cradle hung from its rope in front of their pich—the clay hearth—but it was perfectly still. I stepped underneath it and was almost afraid to feel its weight, but it was now or never. I put my hands on the bottom of it and pushed upward.

It was heavy.

Tanya was inside.

But she was so quiet.

I untied the rope and gently lowered the willow cradle to the ground, whispering a prayer under my breath. Finally the cradle touched the ground and I knelt beside it.

I flipped the blanket back.

Tanya, her eyes closed, looking peaceful. No sign of blood. I put a hand on her neck.

And felt her strong vibrant pulse.

I gathered my cousin into my arms and ran outside.

"My darling girl!" cried Auntie Pawlina. She gathered Tanya into her arms and kissed her all over.

"Come, Pawlina," said Mama. "We'll go to the house. Yulia, I need your help."

Tato leaned heavily on his staff as he came over to where I stood with Slavko, beside Uncle Illya's body.

"We need to report this to the authorities," said Tato.

"It was the authorities who did this," I said. "We passed Chort minutes ago, coming from this direction with a pistol in his hand."

"Report what?" said a man's voice from the road. He was obscured by a stand of trees.

"Who's there?" called Tato.

A balding shock worker appeared. His pistol was raised in our direction.

"Please," said Tato. "We're not about to cause trouble. My brother has been killed. I was just saying we need to report it to Tupolev."

"Comrade Chort carried out the execution," said the shock worker. "Comrade Chorny resisted arrest."

"What was he being arrested for?" asked Tato.

"He's a kulak," said the shock worker. "The surviving Chornys are to vacate this property."

"We need to give my brother a funeral," said Tato.

"No," said the shock worker. "I forbid you to touch that body. A sleigh is scheduled for this evening to pick up and dispose of all the bodies."

The man's cold words stunned me. My uncle, the priest, his wife, who else? How many other people had been killed in today's assault?

Just then a second shock worker, taller and younger than the one with the gun, appeared from the street. His pistol was holstered and he walked slowly as he flipped through a stack of papers similar to the inventory lists that Alice had been making. He looked up from what he was doing and said in a bored voice, "Can you show me where the barn is?"

The lack of emotion in these men left me breathless. There was a dead body lying in front of them, yet all they were concerned about was taking his belongings. We were grieving; we were in shock. But for them, this was business as usual.

"Nyl, show them the barn," said Tato in a resigned voice.

I took the men out back, then stood and watched as they harnessed Totchka to Auntie and Uncle's best sleigh. "This will be perfect for removing the household goods," said the balding man to the younger one. "I'll meet you out front when you're done here."

The younger man got the hay wagon and was about to harness Silney to it when I said, "Excuse me, but do you have the inventory of my aunt and uncle's property with you?"

"I do," said the man. "Why do you ask?"

"That horse is ours," I said. "Our barn burned down and so our animals have been sharing my aunt and uncle's barn until we've finished rebuilding ours. They only have one horse."

The man sighed. "I suggest you get your animals out of here, then," he said. He held up the inventory. "It's all marked down here, but it's easy to make a mistake."

I brought Silney to our own pasture, then went back and got our cow, our ewe, and her lamb. As I went back and forth for each trip, I kept an eye on what they were doing

34

with Auntie and Uncle's house. Both shock workers were going through it and loading cauldrons and pots into the sleigh, but silver spoons and small gold icons ended up in their pockets.

The younger shock worker came out of the house, holding a stack of bound papers in his fist. "What's this?" he asked me.

"Just some notes," I said.

It was much more than that but I hoped he wouldn't figure it out. Uncle Illya and Auntie Pawlina had been compiling our local variations of old folk songs. There were love songs, laments, and kolysankas, but also one jaunty tune that some people thought made fun of Stalin.

"Is this the only copy?" he asked.

"It's my homework," I said. "It's not important."

"Do you think I'm stupid? I know what this is," said the shock worker. "We've been looking for it."

He struck a match and lit the corner, then turned it carefully to make sure the whole thing burned.

The other shock worker came out to watch. "It's good to get rid of this backward Ukrainian garbage," he said. "You should stick to Soviet songs. They're much better."

Anger and grief surged inside me as the flames destroyed years of work. I wanted nothing more than to punch those self-satisfied shock workers. My hands clenched at the thought of it.

But then I thought of my baby cousin. She had just lost her father and her home. Punching these shock workers wouldn't change that. In fact, it might make it worse.

I took a deep breath and tried to think things through. Cousin Tanya would never really know her father. He would never hug her or rock her to sleep again. I wanted to help her, but I had to be practical. They weren't about to give back the house or the items they'd taken, or unburn the songs. Auntie Pawlina could remember and rewrite some of the songs, but there were two key things we needed to get back. One was Auntie and Uncle's hidden grain. I had no idea where it was hidden, but I knew for a fact that they would have stored some in a secret place as insurance against exactly this sort of situation. Getting that off the property and onto ours would have to wait for the right moment. But the other item was something that Tanya needed, something that was made by Uncle Illya.

"Comrades," I said. "I know this isn't the easiest job for you. You're only following orders."

The balding shock worker frowned. He pointed his gun at me. "Go home if you know what's good for you."

"Please," I said. "I'm not trying to make trouble. You have kids too, don't you?"

The man looked surprised at my question. "I do," he said. He lowered the gun just a bit. "And we're all crammed into the corner of one rat-infested room in Kharkiv."

His response surprised me. I had been so focused on what was happening to us that I hadn't thought about what life was like for the shock workers.

"My cousin, the baby, she'll make a good Soviet citizen one day."

He pointed the pistol to the ground "My daughter isn't much older than your cousin."

"There's a cradle on a rope that her father wove with willow branches especially for his only daughter. It's not worth anything, but it's the only thing Tanya has from him. Could you spare it for my baby cousin?"

The younger shock worker stepped out of the house just at that moment. He carried a variety of homemade preserves in a box and set them in the sleigh. The older man caught his eye and raised his eyebrows. "What do you think?" he asked.

"The cradle? I don't care," said the younger one, shrugging.

The balding shock worker rubbed his chin as he thought about it for a minute, then said, "Go ahead and take it. Children are the future of our country."

"Thank you, Comrade," I said, hurrying inside before he changed his mind. My throat filled with sorrow as I clutched the cradle to my chest and walked out the door.

The two shock workers had the decency to look a bit contrite with their pockets bulging with stolen goods. The younger one held a folded lambskin blanket. "Take this too," he said, tucking it into the cradle. "For the baby."

"Thank you," I said. "I hope Stalin's plan works. We all deserve food and shelter."

I walked across the road to my own house, balancing the cradle in my arms, but my thoughts were still on the events of this terrible day. It wasn't enough for the shock workers to kill my uncle. They also burned the songs. Our way of life was being erased. We had to figure out a way to escape before we were erased too.

Auntie wept when she saw the willow cradle that her dead husband had woven with such hope and love. "Thank you," she said. "Every time I touch this cradle, I'll think of my dear Illya."

Slavko clambered onto my shoulders and looped the rope through our rafters to suspend the cradle in front of our own pich, where Tanya would feel warm and secure. Once that task was finished, Auntie Pawlina settled Tanya in, and we raised it up. Auntie Pawlina rocked the cradle back and forth, to calm herself as much as the baby As I watched, I couldn't help but wonder how Auntie would ever get over the death of Uncle Illya. She had lost her husband, her home, and her way of life all in one day. Thank goodness her daughter was safe. Otherwise, that would have been the end of Auntie too.

I had been so focused on getting Tanya settled that it wasn't until she was sleeping that I looked around our house.

The bowl of pysanky had been smashed into a sickening mess of shattered eggshells and glass. Mama made a dozen or more pysanky every year, but they were gifted to friends. The ones she'd kept were very special; the oldest had been made by her own grandmother as an engagement gift to her grandfather. My favorite was the swirly one she'd made for Tato when they were just kids, but now they were all just a mess of colorful shards.

I looked at the walls and realized that our icons were missing, and in the corner near the door, there was no longer our white embroidered cloth with candles and a crucifix. The altar cloth had been replaced by a Soviet flag. A framed portrait of Stalin stood in the place of honor. On either side of him was a miniature toy tractor.

"Who did that?" I asked, pointing to where our prayer corner used to be.

"Alice and her father left this note about it," said Mama, holding up a sheet of paper. "I think she was trying to do us a favor so we wouldn't get in trouble. I'm sure it wasn't them who crushed the pysanky."

"I should bring my project home from school," said Yulia. "Comrade Holodnaya helped each of us make a much better atheist's corner than that one."

Yulia's comment seemed odd to me, to say the least, so I ignored it. "What else did they take?" I asked Mama.

"They took the half sack of grain from the kitchen,"

said Mama, slumping into a kitchen chair and holding her head in her hands. "That was supposed to get us through the spring. About half the food from the house is missing, and they raided the storage shed as well."

"What about the secret cellar?" I asked.

She looked up. "No."

"Thank goodness," I said.

"I need to get our hidden grain," said Auntie Pawlina.

"Is it underneath your manure pile?"

Auntie Pawlina shook her head. "Ours is behind a false wall in the outhouse."

"Timing will be key to getting it out of there," said Mama.

That night, no one complained when supper consisted of leftover kasha, pickled beets, and rye bread spread with salo—smoked pork fat. I had no place to put Manka and Silney, our cow and mare, so they had to stay in the unfinished barn for the night; it wasn't an ideal situation because there was no door and it was cold out. Tato and Slavko and I had to clear out the building materials for just the one night. The first chore on tomorrow's list was to finish the barn.

It was too drafty in the barn for Fluffy and Bebe, so they both had to come into the house for the night.

It was also essential that we get Auntie's grain from the outhouse as soon as possible, so Yulia stationed herself behind a tree where she had a good view of the property. She kept a lookout while I got the sacks out from behind the false out-house wall, and then we carried them back to our property, hiding them above the rafters in the house for the time being.

Since the cradle was directly across from the raised sleeping platform behind the pich, it made sense for Auntie to sleep up there so she would be the one to comfort the baby if she woke in the night. That meant that Mama and Tato got the lower sleeping platforms, and us kids spread our bedding out on the floor, with Bebe and Fluffy settling down beside Slavko. It was a tight fit, but we managed. I just hoped no one had to get up and use the outhouse in the middle of the night because I didn't want to get stepped on.

I had the strangest dream, of tractors and horses at war with one another. I woke up with a jolt before dawn without finding out who won the war though, because of sounds from across the road.

I got up to investigate the noise, stepping carefully over Yulia, Slavko, Fluffy, and Bebe as I found my clothing and boots. I went across the road to Auntie and Uncle's house, hiding in the shadows to see what was going on.

Uncle Illya's body was gone. All that was left was a smear of blood on the snow.

A military truck idled in front of the house, and the grinding of its engine was what had woken me. Thank goodness we had moved the grain last night, as there might not have been another opportunity. As I watched in the dimness of early morning, a young woman dressed in country clothing hopped out of the back of the truck. Someone who stayed inside the truck passed her down a pail and mop and other cleaning supplies.

The truck pulled away, leaving the woman on her own. She pushed open the front door of Auntie and Uncle's house and carried in the cleaning supplies.

I was curious, but I didn't want to scare her, so I decided to wait until later in the morning to investigate further.

In the meantime, I went to the barn and let out Silney and Manka, then checked on our chickens.

It was finally light enough to drop back over to Auntie and Uncle's house without scaring that woman half to death. I tapped on the door and waited.

She stuck her head out and asked, "What do you want?"

"I'm Nyl," I said. "I live across the road. This was my aunt and uncle's house. I just stopped by to say hello."

"I'm Myroslava," she said, opening the door fully and stepping outside. "I'm from a village a few kilometers from here." She brushed back a long tendril of hair that had escaped from her braid and continued. "My husband was deported to Siberia as a kulak, but instead of sending me with him or putting me on the kolkhoz, the shock workers kept me as a cleaner."

"Will you be living in this house?" I asked.

"As a servant, yes," she said. "Comrade Chort will be moving in here. His wife and son will be arriving by the end of the week, and he wants this place fixed up by then."

So the man who murdered my uncle now got his house? The thought turned my stomach. Stalin's plan counted on getting the envious to prey on the industrious.

I looked at this Myroslava, with her work-roughened knuckles and tired eyes. She was a victim too. I couldn't imagine how horrible it would be for her to have Comrade Chort as a boss. We would be having him as a neighbor. I wasn't looking forward to that either. "That's our house," I said, pointing across the road. "We're friendly, in case you ever need help."

"Thank you," she said.

Over the next two days, whenever I had a break from chores, I watched what was happening across the road.

Household supplies arrived, and as each item was brought into the house, I wondered if it had been confiscated from people who had been kicked out of their houses. Comrade Chort came by only once while Myroslava was preparing the house for his family. It was impossible to miss his presence though, because he shouted so loudly at her that we could hear it in our own yard.

At the end of the week, a wagon with more items stopped in front of Auntie and Uncle's house. A woman whose silky green dress glimmered from beneath a fur coat was helped down by the driver. A sturdy boy about my age hopped down on his own.

He saw me watching, so he came over to introduce himself. "I'm Grischa," he said. "Comrade Chort is my father."

Even if I hadn't already known who his father was, I would have guessed it. Like his father, he was tall and muscular, and like his father, his face seemed to be set in a permanent sneer. His mother walked over to say hello as well, and I was struck by how different she was from her son and husband. Her face broke out into a friendly smile as she gripped one of my hands in both of hers. "Please call me Yelena," she said. Her hands had no callouses, and her face was pale. She'd obviously never worked on a farm.

Comrade Chort didn't spend much time at the house at all, and for that I was grateful because when he was there, he shouted at the women and stomped about. He'd also sit outside at the front of the house with a cigarette in one hand and a bottle of vodka in the other and watch the people go by. Seeing as we were the ones who went by most often, it was like living under a magnifying glass.

CHAPTER FOUR
TRAVEL TO THE MOON

My family still ate breakfast together before we all started our daily tasks, but with so much of our food confiscated, portions were small. It was an unspoken rule that Auntie Pawlina got anything extra because she was nursing Tanya. My poor little cousin seemed always hungry, so it was a good thing our ewe had extra milk. Often, I'd sit Tanya on my lap and cajole her into a good mood by feeding her spoonfuls of ewe's milk thickened with kasha flour while I ignored my own grumbling stomach.

Manka wasn't due to give birth until April, so we still had a few hungry weeks to wait until we had cow's milk again, not to mention butter and cheese, although what one cow produced wouldn't go far with seven mouths to feed. The chickens would start laying eggs around the same time Manka calved, but again, we only had six chickens. Even so, the possibility of more food in April was something to look forward to.

Slavko helped Tato and me finish the barn, and we built a false ceiling above the rafters to hide Auntie Pawlina's grain. It was good that our animals finally had a functioning barn, and once it got warmer, I was planning on sleeping out there too. I was used to sleeping through the noises of my own family, but our house was so crowded now with cranky hungry people that no one got a good sleep.

Uncle Illya's death had shaken all of us. He was Tato's older brother and best friend. To me, he was like a second father, but our sorrow couldn't compare with Auntie Pawlina's. To lose the love of her life in such a shocking way and not be able to bury him or have the dignity of the priest's blessing affected her to the core.

Our little family did the best that we could to honor Uncle Illya. Tato made a wooden cross and carved in an intricate geometric design that looked like Auntie's embroidery.

"We can place it in the cemetery," said Tato. "We can have our own private ceremony."

Auntie Pawlina clasped the cross to her chest. "This is beautiful," she said. "Illya would have loved it. But I don't want to think of him in that cemetery now. It overlooks the kolkhoz and our desecrated church. I don't think that would make his soul happy. It certainly does nothing for me."

"Where should we put it, then?" asked Tato.

"By the windmill," said Auntie Pawlina. "I like to imagine him looking at the river, the willow trees, and the orchards."

"You're right," Mama said. "Much better than the cemetery."

Ruslana and Vera came to the tribute and so did their father. The girls sang "Vichnaya Pamyat" for Uncle Illya in their clear strong voices, and they also sang some of the old folk songs that Auntie and Uncle had been collecting in their book. Some of my classmates attended, but not Fedir. After the informal tribute was over and everyone had left, Slavko and Yulia went off to collect firewood, and Tato went to the barn to do some work. I should have followed Tato, but instead I just stood there.

Mama turned to me and said, "Come inside and sit for now. You'll feel better after some tea."

Auntie carried Tanya, and I followed her and Mama into the house. Mama put the kettle to warm in the pich. Auntie Pawlina sat at the kitchen table with Tanya on her lap, and I slumped down beside her, stifling a sob. I loved my father so much, yet here was this little girl who would grow up never knowing her father. It seemed so unfair.

Just then, there was a light tapping on our door. I opened it a crack. It was Yelena, Chort's wife, holding a dish covered with a familiar embroidered cloth. It was one that Auntie had crafted herself.

I opened the door all the way. "Please come in," I said.

She stepped in just far enough so the door closed behind her. "Vichnaya pamyat," she said, her eyes wet with tears. "May you remember Illya Chorny always. This food, cloth, and plate are my tribute to his memory."

Mama came over and took the plate from Yelena. "Can you stay for tea?" she asked.

"No," said Yelena. "Chort would beat me if he realized I was here." She turned to Auntie Pawlina. "I am sorry that my husband killed yours, and I am sorry that I live in your house. If I could turn back the clock, I would."

Auntie Pawlina's eyes widened, but she didn't respond. Yelena walked out.

There was silence for a minute, or maybe two. Then Mama lifted the cloth from the plate and showed it to Pawlina.

"One piece of my stitchwork back," said Pawlina.

Mama held the plate to Pawlina and then to me. Yelena had brought us apple squares.

"I wonder if those were made from your store of apples," I said to Auntie Pawlina.

She took a bite and nodded. "Probably," she said. "And that plate," she said, putting a finger on its edge, "was a wedding gift."

"It was either thoughtful or ghoulish of her to select such personal items," I said.

"I think she was trying to be thoughtful," said Auntie Pawlina. "I certainly appreciate having these mementos back."

A few nights after Uncle Illya's tribute, we all sat around the table digesting a particularly sparse supper.

"We need to escape," said Tato.

"There's more risk in leaving, Stefan," said Mama. "Surely the government will come to its senses and realize their plan won't work."

"You're wrong, Mychalyna," said Auntie Pawlina. "We need to get out of here."

"Where would we possibly go?" said Mama.

"Across the Zbruch River," said Auntie Pawlina. "To Polish Ukraine. I have cousins in Ternopil. Maybe they could help us."

"That's an excellent idea," said Tato.

"That's so far away," said Mama. "We may as well look for a way to travel to the moon."

The next morning, as I walked to school, I ignored my grumbling stomach and thought about what Auntie Pawlina had suggested. This collectivization seemed headed for disaster. Auntie Pawlina and Tato were right—we had to get out. But the chances of getting the opportunity—and means—to leave seemed nonexistent.

I paused in front of Ruslana's house, and for a moment I forgot that she no longer lived there. She and her family had been forced onto the kolkhoz. Now their quaint cottage had been transformed into a storage depot for confiscated goods. A soldier sat on a chair in front of the door, his eyes closed and a shotgun resting across his lap.

Houses all over Felivka had been raided while we were at the village square watching our church and priest be destroyed. Some people had been arrested and sent to slave labor camps in the north, but some people had been killed. Yulia's classmate Iryna and her parents were gone. They had owned the general store in the village square, and it had been taken over by one of the shock workers. A friend of Slavko's had also vanished with his family. Had they been deported or killed? No one knew, but either way, it was terrifying. The only people who didn't get raided, arrested, or killed were the ones who had signed up to help Tupolev conduct the raids. Livestock, people, household goods, and food all vanished.

People joined the kolkhoz not because they wanted to but out of necessity. Tupolev himself said, "It's part of Stalin's collectivization plan. If you want to eat, join the kolkhoz."

As I walked past the village square, I could see the outline of the kolkhoz beyond it. Ruslana had told me that no one was really in charge of the day-to-day running of it because it was supposed to be managed cooperatively, but when people bickered, Tupolev's decisions stood.

The buildings had all been completed and nearly half the residents of Felivka had signed on. There were people milling about, and some of the horses and cows were visible in the pasture. It was odd to see so many animals together because usually each farmer would have just one cow and one horse. I squinted to see if I could find Totchka, Auntie's distinctive black mare, but I couldn't see her.

I kept my head bowed as I passed what had been our church because it was impossible to look at the spot now without getting upset. It was terrible to think of the way that our priest and holy mother had been killed, and I wondered about Roman too. No one in the village had seen him since the day of the attacks. Had he managed to escape? Where was he now?

The only thing that remained of our church was the floor—an ancient tilework of ledger stones—flat grave markers for each of the people buried in the catacombs below it. I had checked them all out when I was younger, and the oldest was from 1690. Now a Red Army cannon rested on top of our ledger stones.

Ruslana was waiting outside the school for me when I got there. "Here," she said, thrusting a coarse wheat bun into my hand when no one was looking.

I shoved it inside my jacket. "Thanks," I said. When I got home, I'd share it with my family. If Ruslana was caught giving kolkhoz food to me, she'd be in big trouble, but she did it as often as she could. "How are things going?"

"Chores every waking hour," she said.

Just then the bell rang, so we all filed inside.

As students around me took their seats, I slid my atlas out from my desk and looked at a map of the Soviet Union and Poland. I found the Zbruch River, and close to it, I found Ternopil. With my ruler I calculated the distance— almost eight hundred kilometers as the crow flies. Was it even possible to travel that far? Could we go on foot, by train? I tried to imagine Tanya making that trip. Mama was right, we may as well try to go to the moon.

Comrade Petrovna looked as tired as I felt as she went up and down the aisles to give us back our essays. We were all supposed to write about one aspect of Stalin's five-year plan, and our marks were based on our enthusiasm for the ideology—in other words, we'd be rewarded for how well we lied. I had chosen the miracle of Soviet tractors at the urging of my brother, and when Comrade Petrovna placed my essay on my desk, I was pleased to see that my blustering had scored a near-perfect mark.

Ruslana sat in front of me, and her mark was also excellent. She held her paper over her shoulder so I could see the topic: "The Derzhprom: How the Soviets Invented the Skyscraper."

Grischa, Comrade Chort's son, sat beside me. He grinned when the teacher handed him his paper. He held it up so I could see that he got a perfect score. I angled my head to read the title of his essay: "An Exhibit Proposal for the Anti-religious Museum of Moscow."

Fedir sat on my other side, and I was curious about his essay topic. Comrade Petrovna got to his desk and plopped his paper down in front of him. He flipped it over to see the mark, but his face looked stricken, and he quickly covered the mark with his hand. I had already seen it though—a failing grade. Fedir never failed, especially not essays. He saw me angling to get a look at his topic. He scowled but held the paper up for me to see. The paper was on how to make a kolkhoz function more efficiently.

The fact that he'd choose such a topic took courage. He was certainly braver than me.

Our next subject was algebra, and as Fedir walked up to the board to show his work for a complicated equation, I stifled a yawn. He and his father still lived in their old house, which was directly across from the village square. It had been fixed up with items confiscated from so-called kulaks and now was one of the nicest houses in Felivka. If we were still close friends, I would have asked him how he felt about that, benefiting from other people's misfortunes.

Their neighbor was Comrade Holodnaya, Yulia's teacher, who was one of the first to sign up as a shock worker. After the priest's and holy mother's murder, the other shock workers avoided pilfering from their house almost as if they were superstitious about it, but Holodnaya wasn't bothered by that at all. She and her husband took a wheelbarrow over and emptied the house bit by bit of antique plates, rugs, books—all sorts of things that had been passed down from priest to priest for centuries.

The lessons droned on, and I struggled to pay attention, but that's a hard thing to do when you're hungry and tired. Just before class ended, Comrade Petrovna said, "There's a meeting tonight. This is for villagers and kolkhozniks alike. Every family must be there."

CHAPTER FIVE
DIZZY

I looked around the meeting hall in the village council building and wondered what speech Tupolev could possibly give that would apply to all of us. Usually kolkhozniks and villagers had separate meetings, but here we were all together. Fedir and his father were in the front row, and Ruslana sat a row behind me with her father and sister. My whole family, including Auntie and Tanya, took up an entire row in the middle of the audience.

Tupolev walked up to the podium. "I've been ordered to read you Stalin's speech from the March second edition of *Pravda*." His eyes nervously darted around the room. He held up the newspaper and his hand shook. "It's called 'Dizzy with Success.'"

I'd seen Tupolev look blustering and angry—bossy too. But nervous about reading a speech? That was new.

The speech itself was long and windy, and as Tupolev

read it, I understood why he was nervous. Stalin blasted the shock workers for all their violence.

I looked over to my father and whispered, "So stealing property and killing people wasn't Stalin's plan? Murdering our priest, that wasn't approved by Stalin?"

Tato whispered back, "That's what it sounds like."

Anger was building up within me. I looked around the audience. Others looked angry as well.

Someone behind me shouted, "So you didn't have to steal so much from us? You didn't have to kick us out of our homes?"

The room became still.

Ruslana called out from behind us, "We want a new priest."

Someone else shouted, "Rebuild our church!"

"This is your fault, Tupolev," someone shouted from behind me.

Tupolev's eyes darted around the room.

"Let's kill Tupolev," shouted someone from the back.

After that, it was pandemonium, with people shouting and knocking down chairs. Half a dozen people rushed up to Tupolev, but Tato held me back when I tried to do the same. Tupolev made a run toward the back exit, but Taras Petrov, my teacher's husband, tackled him to the ground. "You destroyed our community," he said, punching him in the face.

Other villagers crowded in, but Comrade Berkovich jumped up from his seat and blocked them from getting to Tupolev. Fedir rushed up to assist his father, and the two of them pulled Petrov off Tupolev. An angry crowd formed around Berkovich, Fedir, and Tupolev. Berkovich shouted, "Go home now. What's done is done, but we'll stop forcing people into the kolkhoz."

Mama's hand gripped my elbow. "Let's get out of here."

"I want my Totchka back," said Auntie Pawlina to the group of villagers who had gathered around outside after the meeting.

"The mare isn't yours anymore. Berkovich said what's done is done," said a voice at the back of the crowd.

"I'm going to the kolkhoz," said Auntie Pawlina. "Who'll come with me?"

"It won't work," said Petrov. "What if Tupolev calls in the army?"

Mama made her way through the crowd, not with pushes and shoves, but with "Excuse me" and "Please." When she got up beside her sister-in-law, Mama whispered something into her ear. Auntie Pawlina nodded, then whispered something back. Then they stood side by side up at the front, staying silent.

Mama raised her hand. The sight made me smile. She looked like a student wanting to ask a question in class.

Mama kept her hand patiently raised and waited for people to notice her. It took a minute or so for that to happen, but soon the chattering stopped. Mama spoke in a low calm voice, "We have a plan." She lowered her hand, then gestured to Auntie Pawlina.

Auntie stepped in beside Mama and said, "The women and girls will go in first."

A gasp rippled through the crowd.

"But you could be hurt," a man shouted.

"The kolkhozniks won't feel threatened by women," said Auntie Pawlina. "We'll go in together first. The men and boys will follow us."

The crowd erupted into excited chatter. Mama raised her hand and waited. The chatter gradually stopped. "If you're in favor of this whole plan, can you please raise your hand?"

Every person raised their hand.

"Sisters," said Auntie Pawlina, "go home now, get a broom or a rake or a pot. No form of protection more threatening than that. Brothers, bring your muskets. If the women and girls are attacked, we would appreciate you defending us, but if we're not attacked, we would appreciate you standing by."

"Go quickly," said Mama. "We need to storm the kolkhoz now, before Tupolev has a chance to organize a defense."

After all these weeks of powerlessness, there was hope in the air. Maybe we really could turn back time and regain some of our old way of life. I ran all the way home, excited at the prospect of getting Totchka back for Auntie, and their cow and chickens too. And what about her house? I was looking forward to seeing Chort out of there.

Auntie bundled Tanya to her chest by swaddling her snugly in a long floral scarf.

"You're taking the baby with you?" I asked Auntie, alarmed at the thought of my little cousin in such danger.

"Chort killed my husband when I was in the village square and he was at home. I want our family to stay together."

"Yes," said Tato. "We have strength in numbers."

Mama carried her shovel, Auntie carried our broom, and Yulia brought along a soup ladle just in case.

"We only have one musket," said Tato, taking our ancient gun down from its place above the rafter. I took the frying pan, and Slavko found a big stick. We were ready.

As we marched down the street toward the kolkhoz, neighbors joined in, the women and girls marching up front and the men and boys staying in the back.

The gate was open when we got there, and Ruslana stood beside it with her sister and father. "We're not going to fight you," she said, gesturing with her hands for the women to enter.

The women and girls fanned out, some going to the stables and barns, others entering the sleeping quarters and kitchen.

I stood just outside with the other boys and men, on the alert in case it was a trick, letting the women in so easily. I didn't think Ruslana's family would do something like that, but a lot of my neighbors had done unexpected things lately so we had to be careful.

"I found my soup pot," said Comrade Petrovna, coming out of the kitchen, a giant metal cauldron blackened with age clutched to her chest with one hand while she shook her broom with the other.

A woman came out behind her, holding a wooden stool over her head. "My grandfather made this before I was born," she said. "I'm grateful to have it back."

Other women came out, dragging sacks of grain and other foodstuffs, stacking it all in front of us men and boys.

Then Auntie Pawlina came out from the stables with a stricken look on her face. "Totchka's not here," she said.

"My horse is also missing," said another woman, coming out of the stable moments after Auntie Pawlina.

"I want to help them," I said to Tato, handing him my frying pan.

"Go ahead," said Tato. "The kolkhozniks won't think you're threatening."

His words stung. Yes, I was just a kid, but did he have to rub it in?

When I got closer to the stable building, I noticed the pattern of the individual wood slats. Normally I wouldn't pay such close attention to the individual slats, but we had just recently finished rebuilding our own barn, so I was curious about how the kolkhozniks made theirs. Instead of using one kind of wood, this stable had a variety. A lot of the barn boards had been newly cut, but they had also repurposed old wood. I ran my finger along one long dark plank and wondered where it had come from.

As I stepped inside the stable, the sharp smell of old urine made my eyes sting. Had no one cleaned these stables? I covered my mouth with my shirt and took a few steps farther in. There were horses in some of the stalls but most of them were empty, save for old straw and manure on the floor that looked like it had never been shoveled out.

The last stall was cleaner than the others but still in disgraceful condition. I recognized the horse—Magda Polyak's Brody. He stomped his hoof and snorted when he saw me walk toward him.

"How are you, boy?" I asked, holding my hand up so he could smell me, and then giving him a good scratching on his brow.

"I hate that he's here," said a girl's voice, startling me.

"You're Anya, right?" I asked. There were six Polyak children, and they were close in age.

"No," she said, frowning. "I'm Genya. Can you take Brody home with you so he can get some fresh air in your pasture? I think he'll die if he stays here."

"Let me talk to your mother," I said. "Do you know where she is?"

"I'll find her," said Genya, scurrying away.

While I waited, I got some clean hay for the horses and put water in their troughs as well. As I set hay in one of the stalls, I noticed an unusual slat of wood close to the floor. I squatted to get a better look. The slat looked dark with age, but there was something sparkly too—like flecks of gold. All at once I realized what I was looking at. It was a length of wood from the shattered icon of Saint Sophia from our church. The sight sickened me. It was bad enough that they'd torn down our church, but to treat the fragments of our cherished icon like this—it was blasphemous.

I would have tried to calm myself by taking a deep breath, but that wasn't possible in this urine-soaked stable, so instead I pummeled a plain strip of barn board with my fists and said some bad words. That didn't calm me down, and unfortunately, it scared the horses. That made me feel even worse. I ran out of the barn and took deep gulping breaths of fresh air as soon as I could.

"Nyl," said Magda Polyak. "Genya tells me you'll take Brody home with you and help him get healthy again."

"What's going on with the horses?" I asked her.

"The horses from the village were taken to Kharkiv to work in construction," she said. "When we complained, they brought back some horses, but they were a mix of horses from various villages."

"Is no one looking after them?" I asked.

"The job often gets skipped because there are so many chores, and people here don't know these horses. I look after Brody because he's my own horse and I love him, but by the time I get to him, it's often past midnight."

"I'll take him," I said.

"What about the others?" she asked. "They need help too."

Some of the horses were left at the kolkhoz, but only those where a specific kolkhoznik promised to look after them. The rest were divided among the villagers to nurse back to health. The same happened with the cows and chickens, which were just as neglected.

The padlock was hammered off one of the silos, and villagers filled pots and sacks and shawls with grain. Some people who had a place to go moved out of the kolkhoz, but other people decided to stay. Ruslana stayed, and that surprised me at first, but she explained that their old house was uninhabitable since it had been repurposed into a store-room. The pich had been knocked out, and the windows now had bars over them. "The people who are remaining with the kolkhoz are now doing it voluntarily," she said. "Hopefully that means we'll start to work together."

Most of the city shock workers had fled after Stalin's speech was read, but Tupolev and Chort stayed. Smert,

Berkovich, and Holodnaya also stayed because they were locals. Chort refused to leave Auntie and Uncle's house, which I didn't think was fair.

"What I would like to know," said Mama, "is whether we'll be able to work our own fields without interference."

"At least you have fields," said Auntie Pawlina.

A couple of days after the sisters' march, Comrade Berkovich called for a meeting out in the open in the market square.

As we all stood around, Berkovich stepped on a chair. "I was born and raised in Felivka, and you all know me. I hope you know that I have your best interests at heart."

This opening remark was mostly received in silence, although a few people booed.

"The government wants to send in the army to pacify the village. We need to show that we don't need to be pacified. I pledge to you that if you want to farm on your own, please do so. If you want to join the kolkhoz, we can farm together."

Tato raised his hand. "If we farm our own land, will you interfere?"

"If you farm on your own, everything will be like before," said Berkovich. "You'll pay your taxes and sell the surplus. Stalin's goal is that we have a good harvest this fall."

"And what about if we're on the kolkhoz?" asked Ruslana's father, Comrade Olinyk.

"You'll get paid a wage and you'll get fed and have the right to use the kolkhoz facilities," said Berkovich.

Auntie Pawlina stepped forward. "Comrade Chort took my house. My fields have been confiscated too. I demand my land back."

Berkovich looked at her and frowned. "That house is Chort's now," he said. "And the land belongs to the kolkhoz. There's no way you'd be able to farm it on your own anyway. You're not getting it back."

"You allowed my husband to be murdered and you allowed my land to be stolen," said Auntie Pawlina. "And yet you claim to be looking after my interests?"

Berkovich put his hands on his hips and gave her an angry glare. "It seems that no good deed goes unpunished. Chort wanted your family deported as kulaks. The reason your husband got killed is because he fought with Chort. I stepped in myself to make sure that you and your daughter were not deported—or killed. I'm sorry about your husband, but I can't get you your fields back or your house, Pawlina. But just once, I wish someone would simply thank me for keeping them safe."

Auntie's mouth hung open, and her eyes were wide. I could tell that this conversation wasn't going the way she'd planned. "Thank you, Semon," she said. "I do appreciate you keeping us safe."

Berkovich hopped down from the chair and paced, then shook his fist at all of us. "We have to stop this rebellion. There have already been reports filed by the shock workers who fled back to the city, but I've contacted the authorities myself and calmed them down. I told them that everything is under control. If they come here and it's not, we'll all be in trouble."

"I propose that we do as Comrade Berkovich suggests," said my teacher, Comrade Petrovna.

"Thank you, Comrade," said Berkovich. He looked out at all of us and said, "If you agree, please raise your hand."

Everyone that I could see raised their hand.

"Good," said Berkovich. "Let's grow grain."

CHAPTER SIX
SUMMER CROPS

Brody got his own stall in our new barn, and I treated him as if he were our horse. He galloped around our pasture with his mane flowing in the wind and got along well with our own Silney. We also fostered one of the cows from the kolkhoz, and she calved around the same time that Manka did. No one knew the cow's name because, like the horses from the kolkhoz, she wasn't local. And of course Tupolev didn't seem to understand that farm animals are individuals with their own names and personalities. They aren't machines and aren't interchangeable. Yulia named her Smaylek because she claimed the cow smiled a lot. I never saw that cow smile, but I wasn't about to get into an argument with my little sister about it.

Even though Brody wasn't our horse, I became quite attached to him. The Polyak kids would come to visit him when they could, and when the risk of frost was over, Magda Polyak came to get him.

"The kolkhoz needs all the horses they can get for plowing and harrowing the fields for summer millet and corn," she said as she ran her fingers through Brody's mane.

"I thought they were using tractors."

"So did I, but they haven't arrived yet, and we need to get the seeds in."

"He's a beautiful horse," I said. "I hope the stable is being cleaned more regularly now."

Magda sighed. "Here's the problem: Jobs are assigned, but they're not always done."

"Maybe Tupolev should dock people's pay," I said. "That's what Tato did when we had hired hands who shirked their chores."

Magda threw up her hands. "What pay? No one has been paid yet."

"I thought you were paid a daily wage."

"We'll get it, they say, but it will be a single payment once a year."

"Hopefully the kolkhozniks will start completing their tasks now that it's planting season," I said.

"I hope so too," she said. "Tupolev told us that our annual payment depends on the total productivity of the kolkhoz, so we've all got to get the fields planted. But what if I work hard and others don't? We'll all be paid the same."

Ever since we had been able to reclaim some of our items from the kolkhoz and get some food back, we were all feeling optimistic. Add to that the fact that we had cow's milk again, and eggs and cheese. It felt wonderful to be eating full meals again. After a satisfying dinner of varenyky with butter and sour cream, my stomach felt so full I thought I would burst.

Tato pushed back his plate and said, "I've made a decision. We're taking Berkovich on his word, and we'll plant our summer corn and millet."

Mama grabbed Tato's hand and squeezed it, then she said, "I agree with Tato. Everything's gone back to the way that it was. We'll be able to sell our surplus corn and millet and pay off our debts."

"Or maybe with the money we can go to Polish Ukraine," I said.

"But if we can farm the way we used to, why can't we stay here?" asked Mama. "Our families have lived here for hundreds of years."

"Do you think they're going to build back our church, or give us a new priest?" I asked. "And do you think Stalin will lose his appetite for tractors? And for our land? I bet he still wants everyone on a kolkhoz, but it's just going to take longer."

"You have a good point," said Tato.

During this conversation, Auntie had been silent. Mama turned to her and said, "What are your thoughts on this, Pawlina?"

"What does it have to do with me?" asked Auntie. "It's your land, your harvest. What you do with it is your business."

"No," said Tato. "What's ours is yours. You know that. If we leave, we should all go together. If we stay, some of the money from the harvest should go toward building a new house for you and Tanya."

Auntie Pawlina blinked back tears. "You really mean it?" she asked.

"Of course," said Mama. "We've always shared. Why would that change now?"

"Let me contribute the seeds," said Auntie Pawlina. "We should leave yours in reserve."

"What's the difference?" said Tato. "What's ours is yours."

CHAPTER SEVEN
THE TEACHER

July 1930

There's nothing better than sleeping in an open field in summer, with stars above you in a black velvety sky and the chirrups of cicadas lulling you to sleep. That was the reward in the busiest months of summer, when our labor was needed most in the fields. We'd carry Mama's portable woodstove into the fields and Auntie Pawlina would cook our meals right there. Our constant presence kept the birds from eating our new grain. Sleeping out in the open also meant we could start work earlier and finish later.

Fedir wasn't around often because he had been selected as a maintenance worker for tractors and so he was frequently at the machine tractor station or in a different village. But when he was in Felivka, he took me and Slavko to the machine tractor station, showing us all the tractors in their various states of repair. It was fascinating to see how these big machines worked. Slavko was particularly thrilled.

But the tractors still had words in English stamped on them. "We'll be making our own soon," said Fedir. "These American ones are good though. Stronger and more versatile than horses or oxen."

"Unless you're going uphill in the mud," I said.

"Don't remind me," he said. One time the tractor broke halfway down a row and all work stopped for the rest of the day because it took so long for Fedir to arrive to fix it. Often, the tractor would run out of gas or water, and once, it even flipped over.

Silney was methodical, and she kept on moving. She fertilized the field by pooping as she worked. A tractor couldn't do that. I just wished Totchka hadn't been confiscated because we could have used the double horsepower.

"Tractors are the future," said Fedir.

I sort of agreed with Fedir even though I wouldn't say so out loud, but the big problem (aside from the fact that no Soviet tractors ever appeared that summer) was that the kolkhozniks weren't good at their jobs. No one had trained them to look at the overall results of what they were doing. Some of them worked hard but others didn't. I understood how that could happen because nearly all the people who had signed up willingly weren't farmers in the first place, and the people in charge weren't farmers either. It takes a lot of skill and experience to manage even a little farm successfully, and here was a giant farm being run by people who had never done it before.

Once, when harvest was nearly finished, I came back to our summer encampment in the field to find Roman, the priest's son, standing by the portable stove, bouncing a giggling baby Tanya up and down, while Auntie Pawlina smiled and chatted.

He looked healthy, and he was now about eight centimeters taller than me. His clothes were grubby, and his glass frames had cracked at the nose bridge and were held together with dirty white gauze and glue. When he saw me, he passed Tanya back to Auntie and gave me a firm bear hug.

"It's good to see you, Nyl," he said.

"Is it safe for a priest's son to be back here?" I asked.

"Probably not," he said. "But I figured I'd be safer in your field camp than in the village."

"Where have you been?" I asked.

"Kharkiv," he said.

"Do you have any family there?"

He shook his head. "I've been living on the street with others like me who've escaped. We're like one big family."

"You're looking healthy," I said.

"I get by," he said. "But I miss my family and my home."

"You can stay with us anytime you want to," I said.

"Thanks," he said. "But I'm safer in Kharkiv, where no one knows I'm from a priest's family."

"We should figure out a way to keep in touch though," I said.

"There's a teacher who's been kind to us," said Roman, handing me a scrap of paper with a name and address on it. "She'd get a message to me."

I looked at the paper. *Esther Raisman, 14 Chaikov'ska, apartment 201, Kharkiv.*

I shoved it in my pocket.

Just then, Tato and Mama came in from the field. "Roman," said Mama. "I hope you're staying for supper."

"He is," said Auntie Pawlina.

It was good to catch up with Roman, and it was a relief to know that he was faring as well as he was, although it was alarming to hear how he scavenged and begged for food each day and had to find a place to sleep each night. Mama made sure that he had second helpings and insisted that he take bread and cheese for his journey back.

He left under cover of night.

We all had a bumper crop of wheat, millet, and corn. We'd had such perfect weather, with the right amount of rain, that even the kolkhozniks couldn't help but bring in an impressive yield.

Throughout the village, there was a sense of jubilation.

Yes, it had been a hard start to 1930, but we had stood up to the bullies and we had won.

We took our bags of grain a wagonload at a time back to our place and stored most of it in the barn, although some was hidden under the manure pile for good measure.

Tupolev was impressed with our yield, and when he gave us an estimate of how much we'd be paid for it, Tato was thrilled. We had a family meeting to decide our future.

As we sat around the kitchen table, Mama said, "I think we should stay in Felivka and put some of this money toward building a new house for Pawlina and Tanya."

"I think we need to use this money to get out of the Soviet Union and start fresh somewhere else," said Tato.

"But is there still a reason to leave, now?" asked Mama. "It feels like everything is getting back to normal."

"There is nothing normal about our life," said Auntie Pawlina. "My husband, the priest, our church—destroyed. Our folk songs and our heritage—destroyed. If we leave, we can worship again and maybe I can start rewriting the lyrics of those songs."

The adults continued talking, but no one seemed to listen. Mama thought it would be better to stay, while Tato and Auntie Pawlina thought it would be better to leave. Finally, after much argument back and forth and nothing changing, I put up my hand and waited for one of the adults to notice me.

Tato finally noticed. "Nyl, did you have an opinion on this?"

"I do," I said. "I think we should leave. I have always wanted to get out of Felivka. I think there would be more opportunity for all of us if we could live in a free country."

"Nyl, I'm shocked," said Mama. "Would you really want to turn your back on Felivka?"

"The village as we know it has already been destroyed, Mama."

Mama blinked back tears. "Those are harsh words, son."

Yulia's hand was waving around, and she had a frown on her face.

"What is it, Yulia?" asked Tato.

"Why don't you like the kolkhoz?" she asked. "It will take a while to get used to, but I think it's a good idea to do what Stalin says. We should put all the little farms into one big one. The whole village could work together and play together like one big family."

"What I would like," said Slavko, not waiting for anyone to give him permission to speak, "is to move to Kharkiv. I want to build tractors."

In the end it was decided that we would probably leave, but since we didn't know exactly how or when, Auntie

Pawlina offered to write a letter to her cousins in Ternopil and ask for their advice.

Tupolev invited the entire village to the kolkhoz for a harvest supper and dance. I think this was his way of trying to convince those of us who still refused to join that we had nothing to fear. Being late summer, there was more produce available than at any other time of year, and our personal gardens were brimming with tomatoes, cucumbers, corn, onions, carrots, and beans. We had eggs and milk and cheese, not to mention the freshly milled wheat for bread. Each non-kolkhoz family was to bring a home-cooked dish, but everything else would be supplied by the kolkhoz kitchen. "We're one big family, so let's celebrate," Tupolev said.

I sat at a big table with my classmates, and I filled my plate with delicacies from the array of offerings. After the meal was over, we all brought our chairs outside to watch the stars come out.

Ruslana set her chair down next to mine.

"So how is life as a kolkhoznik?" I asked her.

She looked around to see if anyone was listening, then said, "We still haven't been paid."

"Weren't you supposed to be paid at harvest?"

"Yes, we're a week overdue," she said. "It has me worried."

"Your grain and produce are your collateral," I said. "Just don't let them take it until you're paid."

"It's been taken," she said, looking stricken. "And most of what we had left was used for this feast."

"We haven't been paid either," I said. "But we still have our grain."

"Maybe it's just taking them longer to get organized," said Ruslana.

The evening ended with a rousing hopak. The traditional dance started in the usual way with a lot of couples dancing together in a big circle, and then the boys went to one side of the circle and the girls to the other. Groups and individuals took turns showcasing various dances, each competing for applause. The girls' offerings were mostly intricate dance steps, while the boys showed off with athletic jumps and kicks. Yulia surprised me by running up and joining the girls. When it was her turn to take the center, she did a beautifully coordinated sequence of steps and slides and kicks. My baby sister was growing up before my eyes.

Fedir took to the center more than once, grinning and sweating as he showed off his high leaps and squatting kicks. I was a little bit jealous of his talent and that he was the center of attention but did my best to rein it in. I turned to Ruslana and smiled. "He's really good at this, isn't he?"

"A bit of a show-off though," she said.

I couldn't help but chuckle.

Just then, Slavko edged his way into the center and did a hilarious imitation of Fedir's routine, leaping and kicking in all the right places, but incorporating exaggerated mistakes and a perfectly timed fart at the end.

The audience was still applauding Slavko's amusing performance when an unexpected person edged him out by stepping into the center. It was Yelena, Comrade Chort's wife. He hadn't accompanied her to this evening's festivities. She had arrived with her servant, Myroslava, and the two of them had sat off to the side all night, more like friends than employer and servant. I noticed more than once that they were having a very heated discussion about something.

Yelena turned to the musicians and asked, "Can you play 'You Have Deceived Me'?"

As the musicians started the first chords, there was a ripple of conversation around the room; did her choice of song have something to do with her husband?

The dance she performed was beautiful—a classical ballet—and it made me wonder if she had been a professional dancer before marrying Comrade Chort.

After she finished, a somberness fell over the audience, perhaps everyone thinking privately about the people in their lives who had deceived them. Just then, Mama came over to our table, Slavko in tow. "Can you take your brother home?" she asked.

"Yes," I said. "Are you feeling sick, Slavko?"

"I've got a stomachache."

"Your father and I will be coming home a bit late," said Mama. "There's a meeting for the landowners. We'll be at the village council building if you need us."

"What about Yulia?" I asked. "Is she coming with me and Slavko?"

Mama shook her head. "I've given her permission to stay here at the kolkhoz overnight. She's thinking of joining their dance group."

"Oh," I said. It surprised me that she'd want to stay in the kolkhoz, but it did sound like a wonderful opportunity. Besides that, nearly all her classmates were now kolkhozniks.

As Slavko and I started on our walk home, I asked, "How are you feeling, brother?"

"I don't really have a stomachache. I just wanted an excuse to leave," he said. "My friends wanted me to stay overnight in the kolkhoz, and I thought saying I was sick was less likely to hurt their feelings than saying I didn't want to."

"Why didn't you want to stay?" I asked.

"Being with my family is better," he said.

CHAPTER EIGHT
YELENA'S SONG

As we walked, we talked about the great food we'd eaten at the banquet and the dances and songs that were performed. I was so caught up in our conversation that I didn't take note of the truck idling in the village square.

We kept on walking, and there were voices in the air. Slavko stopped talking midsentence. "Did you hear that?" he asked.

I stood still and listened hard.

The usual chirrup of cicadas.

And fragments of urgent whispers in the breeze.

We kept our silence and walked with soft steps so we could listen for sounds. A truck passed.

"That's the second truck we've seen tonight," said Slavko. "Why are they here?"

"I was wondering the same thing," I said. No one in Felivka owned a truck, not even Chort or Tupolev. Everyone used horse-drawn wagons.

As we got closer to our end of the village, we were about to pass the Holotas' house when a third truck pulled away from their barn. Why would a truck be at their barn?

The truck drove past us, and even though I kept my head down and pretended not to look at it, I glanced at the driver out of the corner of my eye. A military cap and collar. The military? That would explain the trucks, but why would the army be visiting the Holotas?

When we finally got inside our own house, I could hear the hum of a motor idling out back. Slavko noticed it too, and he opened his mouth to say something but stopped when I put my finger on his lips.

I crept out quietly, hiding in the shadows and behind trees so that no one would see us. Slavko did the same, but a meter or so behind me.

The side of our barn where our wheat was stored had been tethered open with a rope, and a military truck was backed up into it. Two soldiers were lifting our sacks of grain and throwing them into the back of the truck. All our hard work. Our exceptional crop. We weren't being paid for it. They were stealing it.

I stepped forward and said, "Excuse me, comrades. Can I help you?"

One of the soldiers ignored me, but the other stopped and looked me up and down. "Go back to bed, kid," he said.

"That's my family's grain," I said. "Why are you taking it? And in the middle of the night, no less?"

The soldier pulled out his pistol and pointed it at my head. "Just leave," he said. "We have work to do."

I put my hands up and stumbled back a few steps. "Comrades, I'm asking a question, that's all. We pay our taxes, but you're taking everything, and in the middle of the night."

"I'm counting to three. If you don't get out of here, you're dead. One, two . . ."

Slavko grabbed my belt and pulled me hard from behind. I nearly fell but regained my balance. We ran from the barn but hid behind a tree so we could continue to watch them. When they finished loading our grain, one of them got a burlap bag from the truck and went to our garden.

Slavko ran after the soldier. "Leave our garden alone," he said.

The soldier ignored him. I watched helplessly as he filled up the bag with what vegetables were still left there. I wished Mama and Tato were home. Tato wouldn't stand for this. If an adult ordered them away, would they have listened?

I ran and stood beside Slavko in front of our small garden. The soldier with the burlap bag was kneeling in front of Mama's potatoes. I put my hands on my hips and tried to look like an adult. "You realize that this garden means the difference between my family living and dying over the next winter, don't you?"

The soldier looked up. "This doesn't belong to you," he said. "It's being shipped to the cities. If you want to eat, join the kolkhoz."

His words sent a chill through me. Ruslana said the kolkhoz harvest had also been taken.

And then it sunk in on me just how big Stalin's lie had been. While we were all dancing and eating in the kolkhoz, he had sent in the army to steal our food and grain. He had tricked us this entire growing season, lulling us into thinking they had softened their methods. We provided them with a bountiful harvest, and now they would leave us with nothing.

And what of Mama and Tato at this meeting? They had gathered all the landowners and there was that idling truck. What was happening to them now?

I grabbed Slavko's hand and ran from the soldier. We flew onto the street. Right at that minute, Comrade Chort opened his door and stepped out. He grinned. "Pretty good plan, wouldn't you say? I might even get another promotion."

I ignored him. Slavko and I kept running down the street. We got to the village square. The truck was still parked in front of the village council building, but there was no driver and the motor had been turned off. The door of the council building was closed. I ran up to it and pulled on the handle, but it was locked.

I pounded on the door, shouting, "Mama, Tato, they're stealing our grain."

No one opened it. I ran around to the side of the building, my brother at my heels. There was a side window, but I was too short to look inside. "Boost me up," said Slavko.

"What do you see?" I asked him as he gripped on to the wooden window frame and peered inside.

"Soldiers," he said. "And a bunch of our farmers are tied together with rope."

"What about Mama and Tato?" I asked.

"I can't tell. Stop jiggling," he said, brushing dust off the window. "Okay, I see them. They're tied up. Auntie is not tied up. She's sitting off in a corner, holding Tanya."

He jumped down from my shoulders, then wrapped his arms around me and wept. Sometimes I forgot that he was just a kid. "Was Tupolev there?" I asked.

Slavko stopped crying and looked up at me. "Yes," he said. "But he was sitting in a corner. He didn't look in charge."

"Any other shock worker?" I asked.

"Not Berkovich or Holodnaya that I could see."

Just then, Fedir emerged from the shadows and trotted over to us. "Are you crazy?" he whispered. "If they see you standing here, they'll arrest you. Go home."

"Where's your father?" I asked him.

"Still at the kolkhoz," he said.

"Was he a part of this?" I asked, my hands clenched, ready to fight.

"No," he said.

I turned to Slavko. "I'm going to the kolkhoz to find out what's going on. You stay here so we know what's happening to our parents, but don't let the soldiers see you."

"I'll stay here too," said Fedir.

I ran to the kolkhoz. The doors to the outer courtyard were still wide open, and many of the kolkhozniks stood chatting in clusters. A bandurist played a soft melody from one of the corners. This quiet and contented scene was such a contrast with what was happening in the rest of the village that for a moment I had to stop and organize my thoughts.

I took a deep breath to calm myself, then looked around. Berkovich and Holodnaya were standing in the far shadows in an animated conversation. I strode up to them.

"Comrades," I said, trying to be as polite and calm as I could under the circumstances. "Our farmers are locked up in the village council hall."

"They're not locked up," said Berkovich. "It's just a meeting."

"No," I said. "We tried to open the door and couldn't. Slavko looked through the window and he could see soldiers in there and people tied up. There are trucks all over the village, loading up on farmers' grain while they can't be there to defend it."

A wave of anger passed over Berkovich's face. "Someone's double-crossed us."

Holodnaya said nothing, and she didn't look surprised. Had she known about this beforehand?

Berkovich flew out of the courtyard and around the corner to the village square. I was right behind him.

I had expected Berkovich to go to the village council building, but he walked right past it. He stormed down our entire main road until he got to Chort's house. I stood in the shadows and watched as he pounded on the door.

Chort opened the door and stepped out. "What do you want, Semon?"

"Was it you who called in the soldiers?"

"Of course it was," said Chort. "Tupolev's getting too soft."

"We were just regaining everyone's trust," said Berkovich. "And you've ruined it."

"Look," said Chort. "I'm not going to argue with you. There's a quota, and if we don't fill it, we're the ones in trouble. Now go to bed."

"What about the people at the hall?" asked Berkovich.

"What about them?" asked Chort. "They can stay there for the night. That gives the soldiers time to clear everything out."

Berkovich muttered something that I couldn't hear, then walked away from Chort's house. He noticed me in the shadows and paused to say, "There's nothing you can do. Go home."

"I'm not going home. My parents are still arrested," I said.

We walked together in silence through the village, and as we did, another couple of trucks drove past. It was quite the operation Chort had organized right under our noses. When we got to the village council building, Slavko was sitting in front of the door, his arms wrapped around his knees. Fedir was pacing.

"What did you find out?" asked Slavko.

"Chort betrayed us," I said.

"No wonder his wife selected that song to dance to," said Slavko. I had forgotten about her odd performance after the dinner. Had she been trying to warn us? Too bad she hadn't warned us sooner, or more clearly.

I slumped down beside my brother.

Berkovich said, "Are you planning on staying there all night?"

"We'll stay as long as we have to," I said. "Our family's in there."

"Yulia is still at the kolkhoz," said Fedir.

I had a momentary twinge of guilt. All these momentous things were happening to our family and my sister hadn't even crossed my mind. She had been spending more time with her friends and in many ways seemed separate from the family.

"I'll get her for you," said Fedir.

After he walked off, Berkovich said, "Do you want me to wait here with you?"

"Thanks, but no," I said. "You and Fedir should get some sleep."

Fedir came back a half hour later with a heavy-lidded Yulia in tow.

"What's going on?" she asked.

We told her. She sat between the two of us and looped her hands through each of our arms. "No matter what, we're family and we're in this together."

Somehow, I fell asleep. So did Slavko and Yulia. I woke up with a jolt in bright sunlight when the door we were leaning on suddenly gave way.

A soldier stood there, looking down at us. "What are you doing?" he asked.

"Waiting for our parents," I said, scrambling to my feet. Yulia and Slavko got up too, brushing the wrinkles from their clothing.

The soldier walked to the truck. I held my breath. Was he going to open the back of it and load in the prisoners?

He walked past the back of the truck. He opened the door to the driver's seat and got in. A second soldier walked out of the building. He also walked past the back of the truck without slowing down. He got into the passenger side. The driver turned the key and the engine roared. The truck drove away.

I exhaled.

Tupolev walked out next. He practically ran down the street toward Chort's house. Neighbors streamed out, then Auntie holding her sleeping daughter. Then Tato, and finally Mama.

When they saw us, we had a big family hug. "What happened in there?" I asked.

"It seems they were detaining us," said Tato. "Let's go home."

It wasn't just our grain and garden vegetables that had been taken. Silney was also gone.

Tupolev called a meeting for all the non-kolkhoz farmers to gather at noon in the village square. He stood on the top of a chair and looked out at us.

"First," he said. "I owe you an apology. I said you'd be paid for your grain, yet it was taken from you."

"What are you going to do about it?" shouted one of the farmers. "We need to be paid."

"Please have patience," said Tupolev. "I'll give you each a promissory note. I'll be following up with the authorities to get you paid."

"I can't eat a promissory note," said Auntie Pawlina.

"I'm sorry," said Tupolev. "I'm trying to fix this."

"What about our horses?" asked Tato.

"Those have been requisitioned by the government," said Tupolev. "Harvest is over, so you don't need them.

You'll be getting tractors for next year. There's a whole lot of building going on. The Dnipro Dam, railroads, factories. Construction requires horses."

"We need to plant the winter wheat in late fall," said Mama. "Will we have tractors by then?"

"You will," said Tupolev.

"You've taken our grain, our food, our horses. How are we supposed to live? How are we supposed to eat?" asked Comrade Petrovna.

Tupolev didn't answer. He seemed distracted by someone in the back of the crowd. We all turned to see who it was. Comrade Chort had just stepped onto a chair of his own. "If you want to eat," he said. "I suggest you join the kolkhoz."

A couple of days after the mass theft, we all realized another way that Chort had rubbed salt into our wounds. Our horses had been stolen, but one beautiful sleek stallion arrived. He was named Polit because he flew like the wind, and he was for Chort's private use, a reward for his thorough collection of our harvest, produce, and horses.

When Chort wasn't sitting in front of his house, drinking vodka and watching us, or inside the house yelling at the women, he'd often be seen trotting along on Polit, startling children and chickens, or out in the countryside inspecting fields.

CHAPTER NINE
PACKARD

Late summer was usually the time we had the most food to eat, but with our grain gone and our garden raided, it was shaping up to be a hungry year. I hated to think how we'd manage over the winter if Tupolev never paid us. We needed to leave here and start a new life, but without money, we couldn't get our papers or our tickets.

School in the village only went to seventh grade, so at least I was done with that. I spent a lot of my time foraging in the woods for mushrooms and greens. Slavko, Yulia, and I also visited the orchard as often as we could, scouring the trees for late fruit. Every mushroom, every apple made a difference.

Mama and Tato hunted and fished, and they set up a smokehouse to process what they caught so it would last through the winter. Auntie Pawlina was busy pickling and preserving anything we could get our hands on, anxious to make sure what little we had would keep through the winter.

I caught up with Ruslana to see if things had gotten any better at the kolkhoz. "Have they paid you yet?"

"No," she said. "Our meals are small, and instead of our annual lump sum, we got a listing of our expenses. We were charged for room and board, washing our clothes, and so on. After it was all deducted, we got a big fat zero."

I tried to think of a way that I could make some money, but there were no odd jobs to be had, and even if there were, they'd bring in kopeks, not rubles. I felt powerless.

But then a partial solution came from the most unlikely source.

I came home carrying a handful of freshly foraged mushrooms one afternoon and was surprised to see a magnificent automobile parked in front of our house.

I couldn't help but stare at it because this automobile had nothing Soviet about it.

On its silver-colored grille were the letters P-A-C-K-A-R-D in English script. It had fancy spoke-rimmed tires and a canvas roof that looked like it could open up. The car was covered in dust, but I ran a finger through the dirty film and underneath it was painted a glossy black. I peered through the front window and looked at the polished wood steering wheel, the gearshift, and the leather seats. Was it owned by a person and not the government? And why had a person who drove a car like this decided to come to our house?

Just then, the door to our house opened and Mama stuck her head out. "I thought I heard you out here, Nyl," she said. "Come inside."

Sitting at our table were Comrade Alice and her father, as well as Tato. In the middle of the table was the smallest camera I had ever seen.

I sat down across from them and said, "Good afternoon, Comrades."

"It's good to see you, Nyl," said Comrade White. "I've been trying to convince your father to come to Kharkiv for some temporary work."

"They're in desperate need of construction workers for the Kharkiv Tractor Plant," said Tato. "But I told him that with my bad back, such work would kill me."

"What about me?" I asked. "I'm finished school, I'm strong, and I'm a good worker."

"Nyl," said Mama, coming over to the table with mugs of mint tea, "I don't want you working at a dangerous job like that."

"Here's a map, Comrade Chorny, in case you change your mind." Had Comrade White just totally ignored me? He unfolded a paper map and spread it out on the table for my father, who had already said he didn't want to go.

"Here's Felivka, and here's the road." He traced his finger along the road and then railway tracks. "Here's the tractor factory construction site. You'll see it and hear it a long time before you get to it because it's huge."

"What would happen if . . ." I began.

"Nyl," Mama said, "go check on Kokanka. Now."

Our baby calf did not need checking. Mama just wanted me to stop talking. I looked over to Alice and said, "Would you like to see Manka's calf?"

Her eyes lit up. "I'd love to," she said.

She followed me out the door.

As soon as we were out of earshot, I turned to her and said, "Did you know our priest and holy mother were murdered by your group? And our church was torn down?"

Her eyes flashed with anger. "That wasn't my group," she said. "I can't help it if other activists and the military come to the same villages that we do."

"It was you who made the inventory list though," I said. "And that killed my uncle."

A wave of horror passed over her face. "What do you mean?"

"Chort shot Uncle Illya. They kicked my aunt and baby cousin out of their house. Chort lives in their house now."

"How is that my fault?" she asked. "All I did was note down what each household owned. It was up to the local authorities to decide what was fair."

"Was it you who reported my aunt and uncle's folk song project?"

"I did," she said. "I thought it was very interesting what they were doing."

"You shouldn't have done it," I said. "They burned all their handwritten notes."

"Oh," she said, looking down at her feet. "That's terrible." She was quiet for a moment, and I even thought she might apologize, but then she looked up at me and said, "Everyone's suffering with Stalin's five-year plan, but our sacrifices in the end will all be worth it."

"It doesn't look like you're suffering much," I said. "Driving here in a fancy car like that. You've even got an expensive camera."

"Papa bought the camera used, and it's a borrowed car," she said. "The factory is in desperate need of workers to help with construction so people like you will get tractors. My father and I have been driving around the countryside trying to convince as many people as we can to come to the construction site."

"I would go. We desperately need the money, but your father ignored me, and Mama thinks I'm too young."

"You might be too rude to go, but you're not too young. I've seen men, women, kids, old ladies finding jobs there. I think my father doesn't want to contradict your mother.

He was probably giving your father the map for your benefit as much as your father's."

I was too angry to respond. I stomped around to the back of our house and found Kokanka and Manka in the pasture munching on grass. I squatted so I was at eye level with the calf, then scratched her between the ears. "Hello there, sweetie," I said to her. "I know you don't need me at all. Mama was just using you as an excuse to get rid of me."

Alice crouched down beside me and reached out to pat Kokanka on the bridge of her nose. I couldn't help think that it would serve her right if Kokanka bit her, but irritatingly, the calf seemed to enjoy the attention. Alice looked over to me and said, "I am very sorry about what happened to your uncle and the priest and his wife."

I was about to tell her that the damage was already done, but just then, Slavko appeared.

"Alice," he said. "You came here in that car? Can you show it to me?"

"I can do better than that," she said. "I'll get my father to take you for a short ride."

Slavko grinned. "That would be wonderful," he said.

Alice and her father stayed for another half hour or so, and Comrade White did take Slavko and Yulia up and down the road in his automobile, with Slavko standing on the running board and Yulia sitting in the passenger seat.

He invited me too, but I was still in a bad mood and didn't want to look that eager, so instead I just watched, standing beside Alice, and that gave me a chance to cool down.

"Maybe you think I'm rude," I said. "But our whole life has been turned upside down. Again."

"I know all about lives being turned upside down," said Alice. "It's been an adjustment for me, coming here, all the way from Canada."

"In what way?" I asked.

"When Papa took the job at the tractor factory in Kharkiv, I had to go with him," said Alice. "But I left behind Gramma, and my best friend, Emily, and my swing hanging from the oak tree behind our house. Now instead of going to a show with Emily or helping Gramma in her hair salon, I live in a cramped rooming house in Kharkiv, and we march and make lists."

"Why did you leave?" I asked.

"There are no jobs in Canada since the market crashed. Coming here sounded perfect—Papa getting a job and us helping Stalin build a world where everyone is equal."

"Do you still think it's perfect?" I asked.

She sighed, then whispered, "No."

Comrade White wanted to get a photograph of our whole family standing in front of our house, so Yulia, Slavko, Mama, Tato, and I all lined up. Auntie Pawlina with Tanya in her arms initially stood at the side of the road and watched, but we called for her to join us. She was our family too. We all looked at the camera and smiled.

After Alice and Comrade White left, I realized how ironic it was that she and her father had come here in the hopes of a better life, yet my family needed to leave here for the exact same reason.

Over supper, the conversation was all about the Kharkiv Tractor Plant. I tried to convince Mama that I should go and work on the construction site. We needed the money. And even if I worked there for just a few weeks, we'd probably have enough money to at least apply for our travel documents. That would be one step toward our goal.

But Mama was adamant. "I don't want you to work in such a dangerous place."

Tato looked like he wanted to say something, but Mama gave him a look. And no one in my family argues with Mama once she's made up her mind.

That night, after everyone was asleep, Slavko tapped me on the shoulder and whispered in my ear, "I think you and I should both go to Kharkiv and help build the tractor factory. We'd get twice as much money that way. Our family needs the money, and I'm desperate to see the factory."

I almost argued that he was only nine years old and he'd miss a lot of school, but I wouldn't do that to Slavko.

I knew how it felt to be underestimated. Maybe he was my baby brother, but he was as tall as I was, a strong worker, and as smart as any adult. Besides, we needed the money.

The next day, when no one was looking, I took the map out of Tato's pocket and stuck it in my own, beside the piece of paper Roman had given me with the teacher's name and address on it. Slavko and I packed the bare necessities and left our bundles hidden in the barn. Once everyone was asleep, I set a note on the kitchen table explaining our plans, and we left.

Mama would be furious at first, but in time I hoped she'd understand that we were both doing what we felt was best for our family.

CHAPTER TEN
TRACTORSTROY

The narrow dirt road leading out of Felivka was so rutted from tires and wagon wheels that I wondered how Comrade White's fancy car had been able to get through without getting stuck. Slavko and I followed the road along fields, over hills, and through ravines as the sun rose. The fields had been recently harvested, just like ours, and it made me wonder whether these farmers had been paid, or whether their wheat had been stolen like ours.

As the sun came up, we saw farmers in the field or taking a cow to pasture, but none of them seemed to take particular notice of us; once, the rhythmic sound of a trotting horse behind us nearly gave me a heart attack. I had visions of Chort on swift-footed Polit coming to drag us back to Felivka, even though that didn't really make sense. All we had to do was show the map and explain what we were doing. Working on construction for the tractor plant was helping Stalin's five-year plan. Even a bully like Chort would understand. Yes, Mama didn't approve, but Chort wouldn't care. Unfounded or not, I was still filled with terror, so I grabbed Slavko by the shirt and dragged him down into the ditch with me, pulling a branch in front of us as camouflage. A moment later, through the leaves I saw a ragged-looking man riding bareback. He clutched a small bundle to his chest and looked exhausted.

He was a stranger, and definitely not from Felivka, but his appearance frightened me. Why did he look so desperate? Where was he from, and where was he going?

"We should talk to him," whispered Slavko.

I shook my head and put a finger on my lips. Slavko closed his mouth. We stayed hidden until the man was long gone. I helped Slavko back up onto the road.

"Let's not complicate things for now," I said. "We should concentrate on getting to the construction site."

I had packed a change of clothes for each of us, and we were wearing sturdy shoes, but as we continued, the late-summer sun beat down on us and I realized what we forgot.

"We should have brought our hats," said Slavko.

We kept on walking for what seemed like hours, but the landscape didn't change. I saw no large city over the horizon. My mouth was parched, and I'm sure Slavko's was as well, but the only water we had passed was a small murky swamp that would likely have made us sick and a creek that was too treacherous to risk getting down to.

When the road ahead curved in toward a windmill, barn, and small cottage, I said to Slavko, "There must be a village up ahead."

The first farm was achingly like our own, the house with its thatch roof and the windmill on a hill beyond the barn. As we got closer, a woman stepped outside from the back door, carrying a pail. She set it down at the water pump and began to fill it.

I didn't know her name, so how would I address her? Would I call her *Comrade* or *Pani*? Using *Comrade* was expected since the Communists came into power, but the traditional form of respect was to address an unknown adult woman as *Pani*, and for a man it was *Pan*. A lot of country folk bristled at being called *Comrade*, but if this woman was a shock worker and I called her *Pani*, she might report us for counterrevolutionary tendencies.

By the time we were about twenty feet away, I had made my decision. "Good morning, Pani," I called out, then held my breath.

The woman looked up, startled. She shaded her eyes with one hand, then gave us a smile. "Are you boys hungry?" she asked.

I exhaled in relief. I had made the right choice.

"We are," said Slavko.

"Come into the house, then," she said.

We left our shoes outside and followed her in through the back door. A sob caught in my throat as my eyes adjusted to the inside. The pich, the wooden table, sleeping ledges. It was so much like home.

And then I saw her atheist's corner. She had the same portrait of Stalin like in our house. Yulia had brought home a papier-mâché replica of the Derzhprom that she had made as an art project at school, so it now sat beside the two miniature tractors. She had also brought home a cartoon drawing of a fat pig dressed as a Ukrainian and labeled a kulak, but Mama and Tato refused to let her put it on the altar (I burned it in the pich while Yulia was at school).

This woman's atheist's corner had a metallic bust of Lenin on one side of Stalin and a small Soviet flag on the other.

She saw me staring at it and said, "I just leave that there so I don't get in trouble. I still pray when nobody's around." She walked over to the display and took the items off the little shelf and put them on the floor. She took a bundle from a shelf under the table and unwrapped it, showing me what she had. It was a small, embroidered altar runner and a miniature icon of Saint Sophia. She smoothed the runner out onto the wood and set the icon in the middle, then crossed herself and said a quick prayer. She left the altar in place as she walked over to the kitchen area.

"May I pray?" I asked her. "A shock worker lives next door and we don't dare take down our atheist's corner."

She brushed a tear from her cheek with the back of her hand. "Yes, please pray," she said.

I knelt in front of the icon and Slavko knelt beside me. I said a prayer for the safety of our family and our village, then said another one for our country and all the people in it. I also prayed that Stalin and his people would put the country's needs above their own greed. And then I made the sign of the cross and stood up, grateful for the opportunity to pray. It always cleared my mind.

"Sit," she said, pointing to the bench at the table. "You're hungry." It was a statement, not a question.

Slavko and I sat on the bench, and the woman set down a glass of milk for each of us, and then using a sharp knife, she cut a large boiled potato in half, put each piece on a plate, and set them in front of us.

She sat across from us, but without milk or potato for herself. The large knife sat on the table in front of her.

I lifted my potato half up to my face and breathed in the familiar earthy aroma. "Your grain was taken?" I asked.

"Yes," she said. "Most of my food as well. What village are you from?"

"Felivka," I said.

"You've been traveling for eight kilometers already, then. Where are you headed?"

"The tractor plant."

"Three kilometers to go. My sons are there too, trying to make some money so we can get through the winter." She pointed to my potato piece. "Now eat."

We finished our potato and milk and thanked the woman for her generosity, and as we were sitting on the back step lacing up our shoes, she came out with two well-worn straw hats. "Wear these in good health," she said.

With that, we were on our way.

I knew we were close to the construction site when we began to see more than the occasional buggy or truck, and when that happened, we stepped off the road so we didn't get hit. But once, as I jumped off the road to avoid a dusty black automobile, I nearly landed on a person taking a nap.

The car continued down the road, and I got a better look at the person I almost landed on top of—a dark-haired kid about my age. "Sorry about that," I said. "I wasn't expecting someone to be sleeping by the side of the road." I held out my hand. "I'm Nyl."

"Lev," he said. "Is that your little brother?" he asked, jerking his head toward Slavko.

I liked Lev immediately. He realized at first glance that I was the big brother.

"I'm not little, and my name's Slavko," said my brother, standing up beside me, trying to make himself taller.

"Are you on your way to Tractorstroy?" Lev asked.

"We are going to the tractor factory construction site," I said.

"It's called Tractorstroy," said Lev. "When it's finished, it'll be Tractorgavod, or the Tractor Works."

"Is that where you're going?" I asked.

"It is," said Lev. "I've actually been working there for a month already, but my village isn't far from here, so when I have a day off I come to see my mother if I can."

"Do you mind if we walk with you?" I asked.

"As long as you don't jump on me again, that would be fine," said Lev. "I go the back way into the construction site to avoid the guards at the front."

"I thought they were desperate for workers," I said.

"They are. But they're officially not supposed to hire kulaks, but really, who else would they hire to work on construction? Only farmers will take their jobs, and who knows how someone gets labeled a kulak. I avoid the situation altogether and just go around the back and bypass the guards. The construction managers don't care who we are. They're mostly Americans."

Because we were so close to the construction site, the road was much busier than it had been earlier in the day, so for the next mile we walked through the scrubland parallel to the road, which made the journey even more exhausting and hot and slow than it already was. Just when I felt like giving up, Lev stopped and pointed to the west. "The back of the construction site is one field over this way as the crow flies. We walk straight through it."

Slavko and I kept pace with Lev, and soon we could hear a humming and clanging in the distance. A deep mud pit came into view; it was filled with workers and heavy equipment. There were many horses being used to pull the equipment, as well as wagons and flatbeds. Beyond that was a village-sized complex being constructed in a vast field of mud; that job also required a huge number of horses.

At the far end of the construction was the widest building I'd ever seen. It seemed to take up the entire horizon. There were smaller buildings jutting out from it: one on the left side, and two longer ones jutting out from the right. They were separated from one another by a wide, muddy field. More horses. More heavy equipment. Now I knew why there was a shortage of horses for farming.

Lev made a sweeping motion with his hands to indicate the broad building and its extensions. "That entire complex is the tractor plant," he said. "Beyond are more than a hundred barracks, which is temporary housing for the foreign workers and specialists."

"What about the regular workers?" I asked.

"You'll see that soon enough," said Lev. "We set up wherever we can find a spot."

Closer to us were row upon row of four- and six-story buildings. I pointed to them. "What are those?"

"They're the apartment buildings where the foreign workers and specialists will eventually live."

"I wonder if Alice will live there with her father," said Slavko. "He's a tractor machinist."

Once we were through the field, but before we got to the construction site, we arrived at a vast muddy area where exhausted workers were settling down for the evening. The field was peppered with hundreds of different makeshift dwellings: rags tied together and held up with sticks, a hole in the ground lined with newspapers, a wooden stump beside a clay-encrusted blanket. At each of these dwellings, there were people with hollow cheeks and ribs showing through ragged shirts. Sometimes it would be just one person, but most dwellings had several people. I could see men, women, and kids sitting, curled in sleep, or warming a small pot over a fire.

Slavko and I followed Lev as he wove between the various encampments. Finally he stopped at a mud-encrusted canvas sheet that was rigged up over the top of a strip of cardboard. A kid with blackened bare feet sat cross-legged, stirring something lumpy in a pot.

"Petro," said Lev. "Good to see you're still here."

The boy looked up. "Took you long enough. How's Mama?"

"She refuses to leave the kolkhoz and thinks that we should come back."

A wave of frustration passed over Petro's face. Then he turned and looked at me and Slavko. "Who are your friends, Lev?"

"Nyl and Slavko. Can they stay with us?"

"It will be crowded," said Petro. Then he turned to us. "Sit. I've got potato stew."

CHAPTER ELEVEN
THE WALL

September 1930

For the first couple of weeks, Slavko and I could only get the most disgusting jobs, like mucking the outhouses and the horses' stables. I kept my eyes open for our Silney and Auntie's Totchka, but couldn't find either horse.

I desperately wished there was a river I could jump into because I was itchy and stinky and barely felt human. Slavko, on the other hand, didn't mind being dirty, and for some reason, the fleas didn't bite him. The pay was just a ruble a day and much of that went to buy food, but it was money, and we saved what we could.

Finally, Lev came to us and said, "Good news, two people just left the brickworks. I'll put in a good word for you."

"Two rubles a day, cash," Lev's supervisor, Comrade Campbell, said in stilted Ukrainian the next morning.

"But that kid," he said, pointing at Slavko, "get him out of here. He's too young."

Slavko stood as straight as he could and glared at the supervisor. "I heard you're looking for dependable workers. Try me for a day. If I'm no good, you don't have to pay me."

The supervisor's sunburned cheeks crinkled into a half smile. "You may stink, but you're a spunky one, you are. Fine." Then he pointed at Lev. "Take these two and show them how to mix the bricks."

It was backbreaking work, but a bit cleaner than our last job. A precise combination of sand, clay, and straw was folded into water in a large trough until it was the consistency of cow manure. The mixture was scooped by hand and put into brick molds, then stacked on pallets and taken by horse to an underground kiln where they were fired to make them strong.

Lev had given me the job of combining the stiff mixture with a long wooden paddle. Slavko wasn't strong enough to maneuver the paddle, so Lev had him metering out the components on a scale and pouring each in as I stirred. About halfway through the day, Comrade Campbell stood and watched Slavko from a distance when he came to check on our work. I was happy to see his nod of approval before he walked away.

Our days were long and grueling, but when you work on a farm all your life you get accustomed to that. I was grateful to have met up with Lev. Had he not guided us, Slavko and I might not have been admitted to the construction site and certainly would never have gotten a job in the brickworks.

We didn't have much here at the Tractorstroy, but what did we need, after all? We slept on a piece of muddy cardboard under a tarp, and we tried to limit how many potatoes we ate so we could save as much money as possible. The important thing was that we were alive and relatively free—and Slavko and I were together, helping our family.

I hoped Mama wasn't too upset with us for leaving in the middle of the night without permission, but when we came home with enough money to pay for our travel documents, I hoped she would forgive us. My goal was to make enough money and be back in Felivka before the winter wheat needed to be planted in November. Tato could do it with Mama and Auntie Pawlina's help, but he would try to take on the bulk of it himself and that would ruin his back.

"Will we even plant the winter wheat this year?" asked Slavko. "Once Tupolev pays us for this year's wheat, we'll be going to Ternopil."

"Will Tupolev ever pay us though?" I asked. "It's hard to know if we'll be planting or leaving. The sooner we can make some good money and get back home, the better."

The frenzied pace of construction continued all through October. What struck me most about Tractorstroy was the sheer size of it all. Someone told me that there were two thousand horses on this site alone and this was just one of many giant construction sites all over the Soviet Union. I felt sorry for all the horses that used to be treated like members of a farm family but were now being used like machine equipment. Their farmers would be horrified if they saw how the horses were treated here. More than once I saw a horse collapse and die in the mud from exhaustion.

It wasn't any better for the workers, and I heard that there were ten thousand of us. From those I talked to, I knew that many had fled from the shock workers to come here. Slavko and I had done the same, but we were planning to go back. Lev was the same as us, making money to help his family get by.

But that wasn't the situation for a lot of people here. From what I could overhear in bits and snatches, farmers were slowly being squeezed out of their way of life, one village at a time. I understood now why Alice's inventory was done. The goods taken from us were sold, and Stalin used that money to buy foreign steel and bring foreign experts over to help build factories like this one. It was the farmers Stalin slandered as kulaks who were paying for his five-year plan. Wheat, people, horses. It was all being taken from us.

Those who lived in the mud were mostly escaped farmers, but there were other people at Tractorstroy too. There were the Communist Party officials and elite foreign specialists who lived in Kharkiv and arrived each morning by automobile or buggy. They were easy to spot because they were clean and fat and liked to give orders. There were other less important foreign specialists who lived on-site in a massive encampment of wooden barracks. I was over in that area a few times, and once, I peeked through the window of one of the barracks. Each foreigner had their own slat of wood to sleep on, and bedding too. There was also a canteen where they could get food and a train car that had been rigged up as a shower room, and another for first aid. I hadn't been able to wash since we had escaped from our village, and I could feel the fleas squirming on me as I worked. I dreamed of sneaking into that shower.

Once, when I was out by the barracks, I nearly collided with Comrade White. "Do you and Alice live in these barracks?" I asked him, confused.

"These are only for the men," he said. "Alice won't move here until the apartments are built. She's staying with a school friend in Kharkiv right now, but I've been living here."

"Thank you for suggesting work at Tractorstroy," I said. "Slavko came with me and we're both making bricks."

Comrade White's eyebrows rose. "Good for you," he said. "That's hard work."

"We're able to make a little bit of money, and that will help our family," I said. "When you see Alice, tell her hello from us."

"I'll do that," he said. "And good luck with the job."

Lev said that Tractorstroy had to become Tractorgavod by October 25 at the very latest so that its opening could coincide with the October Revolution celebrations. There was going to be a ceremony with foreigners, journalists, and politicians right at the Tractorgavod.

To meet that deadline, the bosses held competitions. One of the competitions was to mix 250 batches of cement in one shift. There were bricklaying competitions too. Imagine laying a brick in four seconds and keeping up that pace all day? And our team won six onions for making the most bricks in a shift.

As the official opening of Tractorgavod drew near, I thought of what it might be like to be a factory worker instead of a farmer. It would be nice to have a daily routine and steady income, but what I really wanted was the opportunity to continue in school. I knew more about what I didn't want to do: I didn't want to be a farmer or a kolkhoznik. I was anxious to get out of this country and live in a place with more opportunity. Slavko, on the other hand, would love to work here at Tractorgavod when he got older.

I always started early and stayed late so that Comrade Campbell knew he could count on me. Sometimes I got a better job for the day by doing that. The rubles added up.

About a week before the grand opening, the final bricks we made were used to build a massive wall to surround the factory. I was assigned to help clean up all the debris and loose construction materials that had accumulated in front of the factory, and so I was able to watch the wall as it grew taller and wider before my eyes. When it was finished, Tractorgavod was like a fortress, completely enclosed, with the only entry through a couple of guarded gates.

Two days before the grand opening ceremony, Comrade Campbell came up to me as I was wheeling off one of the last loads of construction debris. "You've been a good worker," he said. "And that little brother of yours surprised me too. I'll be sorry to see you go."

"Thank you, Comrade," I said. "I appreciate the opportunity you've given to me and my brother to make a bit of money. It makes all the difference to our family."

"I can hardly wait to get back to my own family in America," he said. "I'll be leaving in a few days."

"So soon?" I said. "Surely you want to see the first tractors roll off the assembly line."

"That won't happen for another year," he said. "And I've got to get back home."

Campbell's words shocked me. "But the grand opening is in two days. I thought the factory was finished."

"The building has been completed, but it's just a shell. There's still a lot of work to be done before the assembly lines will be up and running."

"Another year?" I asked. His words stunned me. "But so much has been taken from the country to build this. How will we farm with no tractors to replace all the people and horses we've lost?"

"I'm sorry," said Comrade Campbell, and he truly did look sorry. He reached into his pocket and pulled out a roll of paper rubles. "Please take this money. It's the least I can do."

I found Slavko sitting cross-legged on a sheet of newspaper back at our encampment, sipping water from a tin can. He looked as tired and overwhelmed as I felt. I flopped down beside him and said, "I have some good news and some bad news."

"Tell me the good news first," he said.

I pulled out the roll of rubles that Campbell gave me and set it on my brother's palm.

"This is a lot of money," said Slavko. "How did you get it?"

"From Comrade Campbell. He gave it to me after telling me the bad news."

"What's the bad news?"

"Tractorstroy may be nearly finished, but Tractorgavod won't be operating for at least a year."

Slavko's jaw dropped. "That can't be," he said. "They took our horses. How can we plant and harvest without horses or tractors?"

CHAPTER TWELVE
FAMILY

Mama was mending a shirt at the table when we walked through the door. She threw it down and ran to us, enveloping us both in her embrace and hugging us with all her might.

"You made it," she said. "I was so afraid that my boys would never come back."

As I hugged her tightly to me, the first thing I noticed was that I could feel every bone in her spine. She seemed shorter and slighter than she had been just a few weeks before. When she held us at arm's length, her face looked dryer, grayer, like she'd aged ten years in a matter of weeks.

"Where's Tato?" I asked.

She looked down at the floor, and blinked back tears. "In the barn . . . working," she said.

Something seemed off about the way she put it.

"Come sit with me, Mama," said Slavko. "I've got so much to tell you."

I left the two of them to chat and went out back to find Tato. He was in the barn, but he wasn't working. He was lying flat on his back in Silney's empty stall. His eyes were closed, and it looked like he was in a deep sleep. I knelt down beside him and gently brushed a bit of hair from his eyes. Gray hair. Had it been gray when we'd left?

His eyes fluttered open, and when he saw it was me, he tried to sit up but he couldn't. "I'm so glad you're home, son. Is Slavko here too?"

"He is," I said. "He's inside talking to Mama. What happened to you?"

"They beat me up," he said.

"Who did?" I asked.

"Chort's men," he said. "They found our seed grain under the manure."

"Oh no," I said. "We have nothing to plant, then."

"Does it matter?" he asked. "We've lost our land as well. It's owned by the kolkhoz. It's their problem now. The only saving grace is that they didn't find Pawlina's grain. That will be for eating now, not for planting."

I settled in beside him and wrapped my arms around my knees. "Do you know the other problem the kolkhoz will have?" I asked.

He turned his head to me. "No, what?"

"The Kharkiv Tractor Plant won't be making tractors for another year."

Tato's eyes widened. He blinked slowly, then said, "No seed, no horses, no tractors, half the farmers from Felivka are either dead or gone. How are they ever going to fill next year's grain quota?"

"I don't know," I said. "But I don't want us to be here to find out either."

"Not much hope of us getting out," he said. "And Tupolev never did get our grain money for us."

I pulled the roll of paper rubles and set it on his chest. "This might help."

Tato's eyes widened when he saw the money. "I appreciate this, but look at me," he said. "I can't move."

"Why are you lying in the barn instead of in the house?" I asked.

"I can't get up onto the sleeping platform," he said. "And I'm not going to lie on the floor all day. At least this way your mother thinks I'm working in the barn."

"Let me help you now that I'm home," I said. "Starting now."

I knelt beside him, and he wrapped his arms around my neck. I gently lifted him up to a sitting position, and then onto his feet. We walked slowly around the barn until his face was gray with fatigue. "That's much better," he said, although I didn't know whether to believe him or not. "Let's go into the house."

It wasn't until that night's family dinner that I

understood the full magnitude of our situation. Mama didn't put a serving dish on the table family-style like she used to do. Instead, she ladled each person's serving with precision into their waiting bowl.

I regarded each person as Mama filled their bowl:

Tato, sitting upright now and trying to pretend he wasn't in pain, but his jaw was clenched tight and his face had a gray tinge to it.

Yulia, sitting primly beside Tato, wearing her Young Pioneer tie and her cherished Lenin pin with the English script. Why was she wearing her Young Pioneer uniform? I would have to talk to her about that.

Sławko, looking eager and happy as always.

Auntie Pawlina, clutching an envelope, with Tanya on her knee. Tanya's hair when I left had been like pale yellow tufts of cotton, but it had grown a few centimeters and it was curly now. She grinned at me when she noticed me staring at her, so I blew her a kiss.

As Mama ladled my supper, I stared down into my bowl. It was mostly hot water with a small boiled potato, two mushrooms, and a slice of onion. She also handed us each a small raw apple.

"I'm sorry," she said, looking from me to Slavko. "We're quite low on supplies since the last food raid."

"This is about the same as what we were eating at the tractor plant," said Slavko. Then he sniffed the bowl and smiled. "Although I must say you're a much better cook than Petro."

"Let us give thanks for this food," said Mama. "And also for the fact that we're all together again."

We bent our heads, and Tato led us in a prayer. After that, we ate in silence, and I let each morsel of potato stay on my tongue for as long as I could. I wanted this meal to last. I wanted this family togetherness to last.

Once our bowls were empty, Tato said, "Boys, it's so good to have you back. Tell us about your time at the tractor factory."

We regaled them with stories about the sheer size of the factory and how many people it took to build it and how Slavko and I got assigned to the brickworks. We told them about all the horses and all the people who had fled their villages to work at the site. We told them about all the foreigners too, and how they were treated so well. When we were finished, I pulled the roll of rubles out of my pocket and set it in the middle of the table.

"We have a decision to make," I said. "What are we going to do with this money?"

Auntie Pawlina held up the letter. "I've got an answer from my cousins in Ternopil," she said. "It's a long journey, and expensive. But they will give all of us refuge if we can get there."

"Here are my thoughts," said Tato. "I can't travel. I can barely walk across the room. But I do agree that we need to escape. I say you all go and leave me here until I get better. I'll follow you when I can."

Mama reached across the table and put her hand on top of Tato's. "I'm not leaving you," she said.

"I'm the man of the house. I could order you to."

Mama smiled at that. "I'd like to see you try."

Tato was in no condition to travel, that was for sure. But even if he had been able to travel, the small amount of money that Slavko and I brought home wouldn't be enough to get us all to Ternopil.

"What if Auntie Pawlina and Tanya go?" I asked. "If they get to Ternopil, they'll be in a position to help the rest of us. Maybe by then, Tato's back will be better."

Tato looked over to me, and his shoulders relaxed just a little bit. "Good idea," he said. Then he looked at Slavko. "You should have a say in this too."

"I agree with Nyl," said Slavko. "Auntie and Tanya can clear the way for the rest of us."

Tato took the roll of rubles and placed it in front of his sister-in-law.

"I can't take this," said Pawlina. "You should buy something for yourselves."

"No," said Mama. "We will all feel so much better, knowing that you and Tanya have escaped these bullies. And once you're safely across the border, you can start writing out the words of the folk songs that you still remember."

"May I say something?" Yulia asked.

All eyes were on her. "I'm not leaving," she said. "Not Felivka anyway. I've signed up for the kolkhoz on my own. I'll be moving there tonight."

Mama held her hand to her heart. "Yulia," she said. "What has gotten into you?"

"It's not what's gotten into me," said Yulia. "You are all traitors. I am bound by oath to report you when you commit treason. Abandoning Stalin's five-year plan is an act of treason. I don't want to have to report my own family, so I ask that you stop talking about this right now."

She stumbled out of her chair and stood up. "Please know that I love you, but I love Stalin too."

She fled out the door.

I jumped up to go after her, but Tato said, "Don't. She hasn't been ours for a long time."

"What do you mean by that?" I asked.

"Who do you think told Chort about our hiding place for seed grain? Now that she's gone, we need to find a good place to hide Pawlina's three remaining bags of grain so they don't get confiscated too."

One bag of Auntie Pawlina's grain got hidden in the floorboards of the windmill. Another bag was sealed within a false wall in the kitchen, and we used the third one for food, grinding it into flour with the hand mill.

CHAPTER THIRTEEN
SCATTERING

December 1930

Slavko, Mama, and I stood at the train depot in the bitter cold to see Auntie Pawlina and Tanya off. Tato wanted to come, but his back was not getting better. He hobbled to the door and waved as he watched us walk down the street.

"I feel terrible leaving you all here," said Auntie Pawlina. Tanya was bundled securely to her chest. Strapped to her back was a carrying frame that Slavko and I had fashioned out of Tanya's willow cradle. Tanya needed a place to sleep each night, and Auntie needed to carry her travel items, so this convertible cradle/knapsack was perfect. And this way, Tanya would still have the cradle that was made with love by her father.

Just then the train pulled up and a tired-looking attendant stepped down. He helped Auntie and Tanya up the steps, and they settled into a seat beside the window. Auntie's face was wet with tears as the train pulled away a few minutes later. We stood there waving until it chugged off into the distance. I would miss Auntie's spirit and Tanya's cheerful babble, but I was so glad that they would be safe, and I was proud that Slavko and I had provided money for their escape.

As we walked back home in silence, I felt the edges of a paper in my pocket. Auntie had written the address of her cousins in Ternopil, and she had also sketched out cryptic instructions of the journey but didn't draw a map. She was afraid that if we were caught with a map showing the way out of the Soviet Union we could be charged with treason. Her notes listed the route by train depots, but she disguised the instructions within a chatty letter: Kharkiv, Poltava, Kyiv, Vinnytsia, and Derazhnya. There was a stop in Volochysk and the tracks went over the Zbruch River to Polish Ukraine, but that was only for foreigners. Auntie Pawlina's papers allowed her to travel within the Soviet Union, but it was better to walk the last hundred and fifty or so kilometers because there were soldiers posted along the border. That was going to be a challenging walk for Tanya and Auntie Pawlina. I said a silent prayer for their safety.

Now we just had to get Tato healthy again and save up some more money. Then Mama, Tato, Slavko, and I could join Auntie and Tanya on the other side of the Zbruch.

Getting more money for travel would be tricky though. And getting Tato healthy again? Was it even possible? Slavko and I had been taking turns helping Tato walk and trying to get his strength back, but the beating had broken him. The only thing that numbed the pain was Mama's poppy seed tea, but when he drank it, all he could do was sleep. Deep down, I wondered if he would ever be his old self again.

The kolkhoz came into view as we walked back home, and I caught Mama staring at it. Was she looking to catch sight of Yulia? I didn't even want to imagine how awful it was for her to be betrayed by her own daughter.

Yulia had quickly moved up the ranks of the Young Pioneers, and she now led a five-girl group of Little Octobrists—kids as young as seven who were given extra rations whenever they informed on family or friends. You'd see them everywhere, eavesdropping on conversations at the village square or in the streets. No place was safe from these little magpies.

At least with Auntie and Tanya leaving, there would be fewer mouths to feed. Slavko got a midday meal at school each day, and that helped, but there was still Mama, Tato, and me. Shock workers patrolled the woods and river, making it nearly impossible to forage for firewood, catch fish, or hunt small game. Thank goodness the shock workers hadn't found our grain and they hadn't managed to steal all of our garden fruits and vegetables. As it was, we lived mostly on watery soup, but without Auntie Pawlina's seed grain and our garden produce, we wouldn't even have had that.

With our animals all confiscated and our desperate need for firewood, Slavko and I had no choice but to slowly dismantle our newly built barn so we could use the wood to keep the pich burning. As the bleak and hungry winter yawned before us, I could see Tato's health fading day by day.

As the end of December approached, Tupolev sent around a notice reminding us that Rizdvo—Christmas—was now illegal and anyone caught celebrating the January 7 holiday would be punished. As a salve to the sting, he also announced that there would be New Year's Eve fireworks in the village square at the stroke of midnight on December 31.

"We'll have to stay up late to stare at that cannon that sits where our church used to be," said Tato, tossing Tupolev's notice onto the table. "And watch colorful explosions instead of gathering together with loved ones to celebrate the birth of our Lord. Replacing Rizdvo with New Year's—a holiday without the holy day."

A night or so after Tupolev's notice, once Tato and Mama were both sound asleep, I nudged Slavko. "Tupolev only mentioned Rizdvo, not Sviat Vecher, Christmas Eve. I think it would raise our parents' spirits if we managed to observe Sviat Vecher."

"But we have no church, no priest, and very little food," said Slavko.

"We don't have our icons or prayer corner either," I said. "And we can't put a candle in the window to guide a wandering stranger to our door. That would be a dead giveaway."

Slavko sat up. "But we'll be together as a family, and we can say the prayers."

"We can," I said. "And those are the most important parts of the evening. I'd also love to figure out a way of doing the meal."

"A traditional twelve-course meatless meal without food?" asked Slavko. "I don't think that's possible."

"It's not about the eating," I said. "It's about giving our parents hope."

"You're right," said Slavko.

"We need to think of what we *can* do instead of worrying about what we can't."

On Sviat Vecher, Slavko and I set the table with the traditional extra plate to honor our loved ones who had died before us, and we gathered a handful of straw from our roof and scattered pieces of it on our table to represent the hay from the manger. We scrubbed our faces especially well and combed our hair in honor of our special night.

As Tato sat at the table, his eyes settled on the extra place setting. His eyebrows rose.

Mama brought over the pot of watery soup and set it in the middle of the table. She noticed the extra plate as well. "What's going on?" she asked.

"Tupolev didn't say anything about Sviat Vecher," said Slavko.

Mama blinked back tears as she sat down. "You're right," she said. "He didn't."

We had no circle of braided bread for good luck. The few kernels of wheat in the soup would have to take the place of kutya—wheat berry pudding—that represented the victory of life over death. We each dipped our spoons into Mama's soup pot and stood, holding the spoonfuls of liquid to our lips. Tato led us in a prayer of thanks. Thanks for those of us still here and thanks for those in our memories. We prayed for a better future for our family, our village, and our country, and we prayed that Stalin would come to his senses. We prayed that Pawlina and Tanya were safe and would soon get in touch with us. We also said a prayer for Yulia, and my heart ached at the choices she had made.

I savored each spoonful of watery soup as if it were one of the delectable twelve courses from Christmas Eves past. I looked around the table, at Mama, Tato, and Slavko. And I was so very grateful for all that I had.

CHAPTER FOURTEEN
RAVENS

Spring 1931

The time between Sviat Vecher and spring was one chilly and hungry blur. I'm not sure if it was actually colder than usual that winter, but I do know that Mama, Tato, Slavko, and I spent a lot of time huddled together on the floor, wrapped in comforters, staring at that portrait of Stalin in our atheist's corner. It seemed impossible to stay warm and just as impossible to think of anything other than food. The glossy sheen of Stalin's face made me think of chicken fat, and in my starving state, his hair reminded me of a greasy blood sausage. Slavko and I took turns going outside in the whipping wind to pull wood from what was left of our barn to use as fuel for the pich, and we also tried to get Tato up off the floor and walking, if only from one wall to the other. Over time, though, he was so stiff and weak that it seemed cruel to force him.

And then he began dividing his daily portion of watery soup between Mama, Slavko, and me. "All I need is this," he said, placing a finger on the mug of steamy poppy seed tea.

"There's nothing in that to sustain you," said Mama. "You've got to eat."

"Don't waste it on me," he said.

It wasn't long after that conversation that I woke up early one morning to a household that seemed unnaturally still. Mama always slept quietly, but Tato? That was unusual. I squirmed out of my down comforter and hurried over to Tato's side. His face looked relaxed, like he wasn't in pain. When I touched his cheek, it was cold.

"Tato?" I said, rubbing his shoulder. "Please wake up." But he didn't wake up. I wrapped my arms around him and wept.

Mama's face was white with sorrow. "Yulia killed him with her betrayal. Putting a knife in his heart would have been no more direct."

I reported Tato's death to the village council, then Slavko and I reverently lifted Tato's body to the kitchen table. Mama washed him gently as we chanted "Vichnaya Pamyat," and I couldn't help but notice how skeletal he had gotten. Tato had never been a heavy man, but he had been strong. Now, however, he was so thin that I could count each rib. We carefully wrapped him in a length of cotton, and Mama stitched it closed with a needle and thread. I would have liked to bury him in the graveyard, but that tradition was long gone. Death had become too commonplace.

When the horse-drawn sleigh came around to collect his body later that day, there was already another corpse in the back—a woman—not in a shroud but in regular clothing. I wondered if she had been beaten like Tato, or whether she had simply died from lack of food like most people did around here now.

"Where will you be burying my father?" I asked.

"Nothing for you to worry about," said the assistant who sat beside the driver.

The man's dismissive attitude angered me. We still had no idea where Uncle Illya or the priest and his wife had been buried. I had a right to know where my father's body would rest so I could go back and pay my respects on holy days.

I waited until the sleigh pulled away, and then I followed it, ducking behind buildings and bushes so the men wouldn't notice me. The sleigh went beyond our village to an iced-over road a few kilometers away. It sapped nearly all my strength to keep following, but I was determined to see where they were taking him.

The sleigh climbed a hill and stopped at the mound on top. Dozens of ravens circled in the sky. This was strange. Birds hadn't been around much because there was nothing for them to eat.

I kept hidden as I watched the two men carry each body out in turn and roughly fling it over the hill. Then they got back into the sleigh and drove away.

Once they were out of view, I ran up the hill to see what this place was. My heart nearly stopped from the shock of it. Rubbish, human bones, shattered pottery, a skull, frayed clothing, rusted tin cans.

My father's shroud had opened from his body being so casually tossed, and now he lay, broken, in the middle of this dump where humans were disposed of as easily as trash, his shroud flapping around him.

Beside my father lay the crumpled corpse of the old woman. Beneath her was another corpse, partly covered with snow. I wondered how many lay beneath that one.

As I watched, a raven swooped down and landed on my father's face. I turned away, fearful of what I might see next.

I ran back to our village with that horrible image seared in my mind. I could not let Mama or Slavko know about this final indignity. It was bad enough that we had lost Tato. I didn't want their last memory of him to be like mine.

When I got to the outskirts of Felivka, I bent over double, gasping for breath. I needed to clear my mind, to calm myself, before I got home. I knew what Tato expected of me as his oldest son. I had to make sure that Mama was safe and Slavko too, but how would I do that?

Once I had caught my breath and my heart had stopped pounding, I continued on my way. I regarded the kolkhoz and its many buildings that had grown like a cancer behind our village center. Yulia was there. The thought of her made me burn with anger. I passed the graveyard where previous generations of our family were buried, but not Tato and not Uncle Illya. My heart ached as I passed where our church had once stood; it was now nothing more than flat ledger stones topped by a cannon. In front of the cannon, two kolkhozniks had erected a wooden display board and were rolling out and pasting a large glossy paper on top of it. I paused for a moment and waited until they were finished so I could see what it said.

It was a poster depicting a cartoonishly fat swarthy man with expensive clothing—it could only be a kulak— and there was a giant fist coming down on his head. The caption was LET US DESTROY THE KULAKS AS A CLASS.

Stalin considered Tato to be a kulak. An image of Tato's corpse filled my mind, so thin and broken. I thought of his clothing, so worn in the knees and hems that Mama had been constantly mending them. Why were we the enemy?

I had to keep Mama and Slavko safe. We had to get out of here. We had no way of making money for the train, so we'd have to walk. It would likely take months to walk the thousand kilometers, but what other choice did we have? We needed to accumulate travel food, and then we would go.

Mama was stubborn at first, but in time, with Slavko's help, I convinced her. As winter turned to spring, she said, "You boys are in charge of collecting as much food as you can, and I'll process it. I'll also craft sturdy travel clothes for us."

It was a dry and cold spring and that made our garden grow slowly, but we no longer had our fields to tend to, so more time could be spent on the garden. Early each morning, Slavko pumped water into our pitcher and watered our rows of potatoes and beets by hand, and I mixed rich compost into the garden to make it fertile. Mama got down on her hands and knees and pulled out every stray weed so our vegetables would thrive.

I went into the woods and picked mushrooms, wild onions, sorrel, honeycomb, and berries. Mama made all sorts of portable food out of this, boiling down the honey and berries into a compact, chewy treat, drying out the mushrooms and greens and sorting them into carrying packs. Slavko was particularly adept at catching small fish and finding birds' eggs. These wouldn't travel well, but they filled our stomachs in the meantime.

Mama insisted that we eat as much as we could all spring and summer so we could gain back some of the strength and health that we'd lost in the winter. I snuck into the collectivized orchards in the middle of the night and picked fruit. We ate our fill of fresh apples, cherries, and peaches, and Mama baked down the rest so it would be easy to carry.

We ate well all summer and the three of us ended up regaining a bit of the muscle and fat that we had lost over the last winter. The plan was to leave in the fall, since the cool weather would make for better traveling, plus it would give us the opportunity to process and pack the most food.

Toward the end of summer, we had a surprise visitor: Roman, the priest's son. I was digging up beets in our garden when he appeared. He was so thin that he would have made a good scarecrow. He was wearing the same clothing from when he had escaped a year ago, and now it hung in frayed strips. His eyeglasses were miraculously still on his face, but I was amazed that he could see anything out of them because the lenses were covered in fine white scratches and the frames were barely held together with wire.

"I went out to your fields to find you," he said. "But it was all kolkhozniks and weeds out there."

"Weeds?"

"More weeds than wheat, from what I could see," said Roman. "Quite a big difference from when your family tended those fields."

The thought of our rich black earth being mismanaged gave me a sick feeling in the pit of my stomach. This five-year plan of Stalin's seemed a never-ending series of mismanagement.

I placed my beets in a basket, then stood up to stretch my back. "You won't believe all that's happened since the last time I saw you," I said. I told him about Tato's beating and death and Yulia's betrayal. I told him about Auntie Pawlina and Tanya leaving for Ternopil.

"At least your aunt and cousin got away," said Roman. "The three of you should all get out of here while you can."

I began to tell him about our plans when Mama came around to the back.

"Roman," she said, "it's good to see you. I'm about to put supper on the table, so you should both get cleaned up and come inside."

Mama filled Roman's plate up more than once as he told us about his life on the streets in Kharkiv. "My parents, bless their souls, would be horrified at how I survive," he said. "I've gotten good at hiding, and at picking pockets."

"The Reverend Father would definitely not have liked his son doing that," said Mama as she ladled more borsch into Roman's bowl.

"Those of us who live on the streets have a code of ethics," he said. "We only steal from wealthy people—the foreigners and the big-shot Komsomol."

"Wasn't there a teacher who was helping you there?" asked Slavko.

"Yes," said Roman. "She still does when she's able. Pani Raisman even let me sleep in her hallway once."

Mama insisted that he stay the night. He donned one of Tato's nightshirts, and while he was sleeping, she washed and mended his clothing and also fixed his glasses.

"How did you get rid of the scratches on the lenses?" he asked the next morning, holding them up to the light.

"Pumice stone first," said Mama. "Then a little bit of baking soda and water."

"You did a good job on the frame too," I said to Mama, admiring how she had painstakingly removed the old wire and had cleaned up the frames, then reinforced the cracked nose bridge with the handle of a spoon, which was held in place with tightly wrapped thread and glue.

Mama gave Roman an old coat of Tato's before he left. "My husband would have wanted you to have this," she said. And she also insisted on filling his pockets with as much food as he could carry.

"You remind me of my own mother," he said, giving Mama a fierce hug.

"Stay safe, Roman," she said. "I hope we'll see you again."

Not long after Roman's visit, while I was picking mushrooms in the woods, I happened upon Fedir, who was resting on a fallen log, his mushroom sack beside him.

"Sit," he said, pointing to the log.

"I haven't seen you for a long time," I said, settling

down beside him. "You must be busy these days, fixing tractors."

"There's a lot of them to fix," he said. "Although most aren't fixable. We don't have the replacement parts, and a lot of them have rusted out."

"It will be better when they're finally made in Kharkiv," I said.

"I hope you're right," he said. "Although I don't know if the kolkhoz will even last that long."

"What do you mean?" I asked.

"The kolkhozniks aren't farmers," said Fedir. "Plowing and planting was done haphazardly. We'll be far short of our wheat requisitions for this year. Stalin thinks we have two thousand bushels here. That's what they took last year, and we kept two hundred bushels to feed the kolkhoz."

"How much do you estimate you harvested?" I asked.

"Six hundred bushels. Total."

"You can only give them four hundred bushels when they're expecting two thousand? Stalin won't be happy."

"It's going to be bad," said Fedir.

"It's Stalin's own fault," I said. "Maybe this will teach him a lesson."

"It never works that way, as you know," said Fedir. "Stalin will blame it on those mythical creatures, the kulaks, and we will all suffer."

CHAPTER FIFTEEN
CUDGEL

October 1931

We were packed up and ready to go. Mama had sewn inner pockets in the lining of each of our coats so we could carry all sorts of food items without using our hands. She had also crafted each of us a sling out of a wide scarf to carry more food, a change of clothing, and essential items. Of the sacks of grain from Pawlina, all that was left was half of one sack, and we had divvied that up evenly between the three of us.

"I'll miss our home," said Mama, as she leaned against the pich one last time.

"Maybe we'll be able to come back here one day," I said. "After Stalin comes to his senses."

"I won't be holding my breath for that to happen," said Slavko.

"One last hug before we leave this home forever," said Mama, opening her arms wide. I snuggled into one of her shoulders and Slavko did the same, and we wrapped our arms around one another's waists. How I wished Tato were with us, that we could have made this escape together. I hugged Mama and Slavko fiercely and said a prayer of thanks. Whatever the future held, I knew it would be a challenge. But I was thankful for what I had, and I was grateful for every minute I had already been given with my family. My biggest regret was that Yulia wasn't with us. Maybe in the future she would change her mind and she'd want to be part of our family again.

When we stepped out of the door to embark on our journey, I had an odd feeling in the pit of my stomach. Something was off.

Then I noticed Chort at his front step, deep in conversation with a Red Army soldier. The soldier leaned on the handle of an unusual weapon—a cudgel of some sort. It was the shape of an oversized hammer with a large club and a long handle; the look of it filled me with dread.

Chort looked up from the conversation and saw us standing in our doorway. He tapped the soldier's shoulder and pointed to us. The soldier turned. He picked up his weapon and walked in our direction.

My heart pounded. "Let's get back inside the house," I

said, opening the door and shoving Mama and Slavko in ahead of me.

As we scrambled in, Mama said, "We need to stay calm." She sat down at the table and pasted a composed expression onto her face.

The door burst open and the soldier strode in. "Where's your grain?" he shouted, holding the cudgel high.

"Comrade," said Mama in a controlled voice. "Our land was confiscated a year ago and was farmed by the kolkhozniks. They're the ones to get grain from, not us."

"You're a lying kulak," said the soldier. "I can tell by looking at you that you've been eating."

He lifted the cudgel above his head and let it come down hard onto our table, splitting the wooden top in half. Mama jumped up and backed against the wall.

Splinters from the tabletop flew across the room. Underneath was the storage space, but since we were leaving, it was empty.

"You've probably got it hidden in the pich," he said.

Slavko and I stepped in front of Mama to protect her as the soldier lifted his cudgel into the air again. He hit our pich with all his strength again and again and sharp shards of painted plaster exploded throughout the house. We huddled around Mama, trying to protect her from the flying shards.

"Nothing here," said the soldier. "But I'm going to find your hiding place."

He smashed our cooking pot and drinking glasses. He found empty jars and smashed them too. He knelt onto our dirt floor and smashed around some more, but all he managed to do was make our floor into a fine dry powder. He coughed and sputtered.

"You got off lightly." He strode to the door and was about to open it when he turned around. He looked at the three of us, each wearing winter coats in October. Each with a bulky scarf bundled diagonally over our coat. He pointed. "Take those off," he said.

He confiscated our travel food and grain. Then he gripped Mama by the lapels of her coat and dragged her out the door.

Slavko and I followed behind as he took her to the kolkhoz. "I haven't done anything wrong," she shouted. "What are you doing to me?"

"Kolkhoz jail," he said. "You're guilty of hoarding food." He turned to us. "Go home."

Mama was in jail for two weeks, and we were not allowed to see her. I wondered whether Yulia went to visit her and whether that would be a good thing or not. Those two weeks were the longest of my life. Slavko and I cleared away the shards of table and pich as best we could and slept on the hard floor, bundled in our ripped coats, waiting for word of Mama. We had no food, no utensils, not even a pitcher to pump water into. Once, out of desperation, I crept into Chort's barn and stole feed from Polit, his stallion. I wanted to share it with Slavko, but he refused it and that turned out to be a wise decision because eating that feed made me vomit.

Myroslava, Chort's servant, must have seen me take the feed, because from then on she left generous table scraps on their compost heap each night. She also threw away a perfectly good drinking glass and a water pitcher one night—a kindness Chort would have beaten her for if he knew.

When Mama was finally let out of jail, her face was mottled and yellow from old bruises, and her scalp was caked with blood, but that wasn't the worst of it. She had a wild look in her eyes that wouldn't go away. And she had strange screaming nightmares. The pich was in shambles so she couldn't sleep up there and it was just as well because she could have fallen off with those nightmares. She slept between Slavko and me on the floor, and we did our best to calm her, but nothing really worked.

We couldn't travel with her like this. We were trapped. Fall slowly crept forward into a cold and killing winter. December gave way to January, but still Mama was no better. Would we make it to the spring?

CHAPTER SIXTEEN
WINTERKILL

March 1932

Hours before dawn, Mama stood in the doorway of our home.

I gasped at how thin she had gotten. I knew that all three of us had dwindled since Mama was imprisoned, but it wasn't until I saw her silhouette in the moonlight that I realized just how close to death she was.

I pushed myself up from the floor. "Mama, where are you going?"

She held a finger to her lips, then pointed to Slavko, whose hollow eyes were finally closed in an exhausted sleep. "To the fields, son."

"Mama, it's just cold hard seeds."

She turned. "We need to eat."

"You'll be arrested."

"If I get caught."

If she walked through town to get to our old wheat field in this frenzied state, she'd be shot for sure, so I clasped her elbow and we went together to a closer field. You could get to this one by walking behind our house and away from town instead of through it. Someone else had been here first, scrabbling through the mud to eat the hard kernels. When we got to the edge of the field, Mama fell to her knees and began to squeeze the icy mud through her hands, looking for one hard nugget of sustenance at a time. I kept a lookout while she dropped kernels into the deep pocket of her skirt.

All at once, horse's hooves pounded in our direction. I gave a low whistle. Mama turned. I flailed my arms. "Hide," I mouthed.

But she ignored me. She squeezed more mud, looking for those elusive seeds.

A sharp bang.

And again.

Mama collapsed into the black earth.

I stood in shock. The pounding of hooves got louder. I wanted to run to Mama—to see if I could save her—but the horseman was nearly upon me, and I knew what Mama would want. She'd want Slavko and me to survive. I sank to the ground and rolled under a tree trunk.

As the man galloped past, shotgun in hand, I poked my head out to see who it was. Chort, of course. He'd go to our house now, looking to kill me and Slavko.

I stayed by the log, waiting for my heart to stop pounding. I was just about to get up when there was a second set of hoofbeats, and then another gunshot.

I grabbed some twigs as camouflage and poked my head up as far as I dared. A man on a horse was chasing Chort. He lifted his shotgun again, aimed, and pulled the trigger. Chort jolted, then slumped forward on his saddle. His body slid to the ground. Polit galloped off.

The second shooter tugged on his reins, and his horse stopped. He was close to where Mama had fallen. As he slipped off his horse to examine her, I ran into the field. Mama had fallen face-first into the field. I felt her neck for a pulse, but there was none. I turned her over. Seeds fell from her hand. I gathered them up and put them in my pocket.

"Your mother?" asked the second horseman, crouching beside me.

I nodded, then said, "They'll blame me for Chort's death."

"I'm sorry, boy," he said. "Get out of here while you still can."

"Who are you?" I asked. The man was gaunt and barefoot like me, and his clothing was ragged. I knew everyone around here; he was not a local.

"A farmer like you," he said. "On the run."

The farmer raked his fingers through the mud, looking for a few kernels for himself. When he had a dozen or so, he got back on his horse and rode away.

I would have liked to bury my mother, to say a prayer for her soul, but she was dead, and she would want Slavko and me to live. I hurried back to our home and woke Slavko up.

"Where's Mama?" asked Slavko, his eyes looking huge with hunger.

"Shot dead," I said.

He scrambled to his feet. "It's not possible," he said. "Take me to her. I need to help."

"No," I said. "Right now, we have to get out of here or we'll be killed too."

It is not an easy thing to force brute sorrow and rage out of your thoughts. My mother lay in a muddy field, murdered. We had no time to mourn her, to say goodbye. All I could do was urge my brother not to think or feel, but to just get ready so we could leave.

We dressed in layers and wore our boots. I felt in my pants pocket to make sure I had the paper with Pani Raisman's address to lead us to Roman, plus the notes showing how to get to Auntie's family in Ternopil.

"How can we get to Ternopil?" asked Slavko. "We have no money, no food."

"Right now, let's concentrate on getting out of Felivka," I said.

Slavko's eyes filled with tears. "We're all that's left of our family now."

I wrapped my arms around him and squeezed him tight. "I promise to do everything I can to keep you safe."

He hugged me back, then inhaled a jagged breath. "I know you will," he said. "And I'll do everything I can to keep you safe too."

I opened the door and was about to step out when Yelena, Chort's wife, pushed me back in and stepped in herself, closing the door behind her.

She was wearing a long, silky green robe that was tied with a ribbon at the waist. Her face was streaked with tears but she didn't look sad. "Thank you for killing my devil of a husband," she said. Then she reached into the pocket of her robe and pulled out a parchment-wrapped packet the size of my palm. "That's some food. Now go."

I wanted to say something, to thank her, but she left before the words came out of my mouth.

"Come on," I said to Slavko. I put the package into my coat pocket, and we were gone.

CHAPTER SEVENTEEN
SALO

Someone must have heard the shots when Mama and Chort were killed, but the only people in our village who weren't starving were those who were in charge of stealing food. When you're starving, you don't have very much curiosity. Those of our neighbors still alive were probably huddled for warmth under blankets, not caring to investigate gunshots in the distance.

Chort was dead, but we still had to watch out for Smert. We also had to watch out for the brutal reinforcements that had recently arrived from Moscow.

Slavko and I darted from shadow to shadow, but the street was quiet and the windows remained darkened in the early dawn. As we passed each thatch-roof cottage, I thought of the people who used to live there. Some had been sent to Siberia or executed. Others had escaped. Some had starved to death. Those who were left were mostly on the kolkhoz now, but they were nearly as hungry as the rest of us.

We passed the village square, and the kolkhoz beyond it. No windows were lit.

I thought of Yulia, sound asleep in the kolkhoz barrack, unaware that our mother had been murdered. Would she be told? Would she care? My heart raged at the person my sister had become.

When we got out of Felivka, I automatically turned east, toward the train station and Kharkiv, on the narrow dirt road. We didn't talk, we just walked as quickly as we could, putting distance between us and the bodies of Mama and Chort lying in the field.

We trudged on and on, and the sun rose, revealing dirt and melting snow on either side of the road. I wondered if these fields would ever be sown or whether hungry farmers would eat the seeds out of desperation before they hit the ground.

We kept on walking, but with each step farther from Felivka, I could feel my feet getting heavier. It had been the energy of fear that propelled us forward at the start, but now hunger and sadness weighed us down. I looked over at Slavko, at his hollow eyes and cheeks. Our whole plan to get to Ternopil seemed impossible.

"Are we going to the tractor plant?" asked Slavko, looking hopeful.

That wasn't a bad idea. "Do you want to?" I asked him.

"Yes," he said. "Maybe they're making tractors there now. Maybe we can get jobs."

"That's a good idea," I said. An excellent short-term plan, in fact. If we could get jobs, we'd get paid. Maybe we'd be able to afford the train for part of our journey.

We trudged on until the sun was directly overhead. This past winter of deprivation had taught us both a lot about surviving hunger. We learned the hard way that when you were already close to starvation, it was crucial to eat at least one mouthful of food every single day. If you skipped a day, your stomach and legs would start to swell. If you waited too long for a bite of food once the swelling started, you wouldn't be able to hold down what you ate, and then you would die. Our last mouthful of food had been at suppertime yesterday, but we had been exerting ourselves today. It was important that we eat something soon.

I pointed up ahead. "Do you recognize where we are?"

The road curved in toward the rubble of a destroyed windmill, a fallen barn, and a small cottage.

"The kind woman who gave us the straw hats," said Slavko. "That's her place up ahead. I hope she's okay." But as we got closer to the cottage, it looked to be abandoned. The back door had one hinge broken and was flapping loose. The water pail sat on its side, partly covered in old snow. Slavko pulled at the warped wooden door and stuck his head in. "Hello?" he called out. His voice echoed in the emptiness.

We stepped inside. The air smelled stale, but it was too shadowed to see much. I pulled open the curtain and gasped. Much like our own home, the woman's table and pich had been smashed to small pieces. The only thing not destroyed was her atheist's corner, with the portrait of Stalin plus the bust of Lenin and the Soviet flag.

Slavko walked up to it and brushed the items off the corner with a single sweeping motion of his arm. Then he crouched in front of it and stuck his hand in the little shelf underneath. He pulled out a small bundle and held it up to me with a smile. He unwrapped it, showing me the small, embroidered altar runner and a miniature icon of Saint Sophia. He smoothed the runner out onto the wood and set the icon in the middle. "At least this wasn't destroyed," he said.

The two of us knelt in front of the altar and said a prayer for the woman and a prayer for Mama. We left the altar in place.

I found her straw broom and cleared away some rubble. I sat down on the floor, leaning against the wall, and Slavko slid down beside me. I held Yelena's package in my hand and Slavko leaned his head on my shoulder. We should have eaten right then, but exhaustion took over. We fell asleep.

I don't know how long I slept for, but when I woke up my hands were empty. I had a moment of panic, but then saw the little package under my knees. I picked it up and held it to my face, inhaling its rich, smoky scent. I shook Slavko's shoulder. His eyes opened.

"Let's see what Yelena packed in here," I said, untying the string around the paper. The smoky scent intensified, and my stomach churned with hunger. I opened the paper and nearly wept. "Look what we've got," I said to Slavko.

"Salo?" he said. "Oh my. Hello, old friend."

Chort had been getting food packages from Moscow while the rest of us were left starving. Salo, the delectably creamy white pork fat, was delicious spread on bread with slivers of fresh garlic, or melted and drizzled on potatoes or vegetables. This piece had been smoke cured, which made it even tastier but also meant it was well preserved and good for travel. Before the hunger, salo was an everyday ingredient. Mama even used unsmoked salo in bread and sweets. "Take a small bite," I said. "But not too much. It's rich, and we haven't been eating and you don't want to get sick."

Slavko bit off a corner of the salo and held it in his mouth. The expression on his face was pure bliss. I took a small bite myself and savored the smoky richness as it melted on my tongue. This gift from Yelena had probably saved our lives. One bite a day would stave off starvation, and the piece that she gave us would last several days.

"I hope Yelena will be okay," I said. "What do you think will happen to her now? And to her son and her servant?"

"It's hard to know," said Slavko. "But they're definitely better off without that devil Chort."

I wrapped the salo back up in paper and retied the string. "Let's drink some water from the pump and then be on our way."

We walked through the village in midafternoon but didn't pass a single soul. Even the village square looked empty and abandoned. A billboard had been erected since the last time we had been through this way, but the poster looked like it had been there all winter because it was weathered and torn. It depicted one group of men beating another group with hammers and clubs. The caption was WE SMITE LAZY WORKERS. Dark Soviet humor. I thought of that soldier who had come to our home and had smashed everything with a cudgel. Soldiers must have come to this village as well. Villagers were punished for being alive, not for being lazy. But where were they now?

We kept on walking.

We passed another village and another, but they seemed dead as well. We kept on walking, but then I wrinkled my nose at the smell of rot. The stench got stronger as we continued down the road. I covered my face with my hand and Slavko did the same, but we kept on walking.

A dead horse, stomach bulging with decay and covered with buzzing flies, was splayed across the road. Slavko and I had to walk into the brush to get around it, and I covered my face the whole time, but the stink was unavoidable.

A while later, more smell. This time it was a man, dead at the side of the road. His legs and arms like brittle old sticks. He had collapsed of hunger in midstep and never got up. Flies buzzed around him.

"We can't just leave him here," said Slavko.

I thought of Tato's body, thrown casually on that garbage heap. Of Mama's in the field. "You're right," I said. "No one deserves such indignity. But what can we do?"

"Even just a prayer," said Slavko.

"A symbolic burial too," I said, bending down to the road and scooping up a handful of soil. I sprinkled it over the corpse and we stood side by side and prayed. As we chanted "Vichnaya Pamyat," I was overcome with sorrow. I clutched Slavko and the two of us wept. There had been no opportunity to properly mourn Tato when he died, and for poor Mama, it was even worse. We had just given this stranger a more respectful funeral than either Mama or Tato had received, but in a way, we were mourning and honoring them all.

When we had no tears left, I put my arm around my brother and we continued our journey.

I felt like a sleepwalker as we trudged down the rutted mud road, passing one dead village after another. Weak from hunger, we took shelter in an abandoned home in one of the villages to rest for a bit and regain some strength. Slavko took a bite of the salo and so did I, and I savored every moment as the rich flavor filled my mouth. We drank water from the well, then started back on our journey.

I am ashamed to say that we got so used to dead bodies that we didn't stop and pray anymore but just stepped over them. I kept my eyes down and concentrated on just going forward.

"Look up ahead," said Slavko.

I was almost afraid to look up, but I followed where my brother's finger pointed. We had just crested a small rise, so we had a good view of the road up ahead. There were people on the road.

"Two adults," I said. "And maybe a child?" I squinted to get a better look.

"Should we hide from them?" asked Slavko.

"I don't know," I said. "Let's wait until we get closer, and then we can decide."

Once we were closer, it was clear that the stick-thin man leaning heavily on a cane was no threat. The young woman carrying a baby on her back wasn't a threat either. She held the hand of a small, barefoot boy who limped along in the freezing mud beside her.

"They're just like us," said Slavko.

"Hello," I called.

The woman turned and so did the boy, but the man just kept walking slowly forward. "What do you want?" she called back.

"Nothing," I said. "We didn't want to scare you by sneaking up on you."

She nodded, then turned. The boy did the same. They trudged slowly forward.

We caught up to them not long after that, but the road was too narrow to walk beside them so they stopped to let us pass. "I'm Nyl, and this is my brother, Slavko," I said. "We're from Felivka, a village about ten kilometers from here."

The man seemed unaware that I had even spoken; he just looked off into the field. The woman's eyes were puffy from lack of food, and her cheeks were hollow. "We've been walking for two days," she said. "Do you know how far it is to Kharkiv?"

"The tractor plant is under two kilometers up ahead," I said. "The city is ten kilometers beyond that. When you get to the plant, take the paved road into Kharkiv."

The old man stopped. "Ten kilometers?" he said. "We'll be dead before then."

"Tato," said the woman. "Let's be hopeful. We'll get there."

I tried to piece together what this family would have looked like before they had their food taken. The old man was "Tato"—the woman's father. Had he lost his wife to hunger or deportation? And the woman, how had she lost her husband? Her baby and child were both in sorry shape and were not close in age. Perhaps this family had lost children as well as spouses.

If they got to the tractor plant, would either of them be strong enough to work? But would it be any better in Kharkiv itself, even if they were strong enough to get there? My heart ached for their fate.

We picked up our pace and soon we were well past them, but up ahead were two girls in dusty coats, holding hands. As we walked closer, I noticed that their feet were wrapped in strips of cloth, and I could only imagine how cold and sore they were.

"How long have you been on the road?" asked Slavko as the girls paused for a moment to speak with us as we passed.

"A few days," answered one of the girls. "Just before Mama died, she urged us to leave for Kharkiv. There's supposed to be food there."

It was a nightmarish walk to the tractor plant, witnessing hungry villagers on the move for food and shelter just like us. Some were barely alive but were somehow walking; others had collapsed but still breathed, and others had succumbed to death and lay there in the road. It felt so cold and soulless to step over these people and continue on.

Death had become too common to react to, and that was horrifying in itself.

Finally we reached the familiar stretch of scrubland that was on the outskirts of the tractor plant. As I stood there beside my brother, I did a slow turn to take it all in.

When we had been here before, the encampments had

been right up close to the construction site. Now they were farther away from the factory complex, but they had also grown in size. They encompassed a wide ribbon of the scrubland and wild area that circled the factory.

Grass covered the strip of land where the encampments had been, and the wide lawn acted as a visual barrier between the vast swathe of current encampments and the apartment building complex for foreigners and specialists. From where we stood, I counted eight six-story buildings with balconies, and there were likely more behind those ones that I couldn't see. There were streets, walkways, and courtyards throughout the complex.

"They were just finishing all these when we were here before," said Slavko.

"I wonder if Alice and her father now live in one of these buildings."

"Good luck finding them," said Slavko. "Hundreds of families must live here."

There had to be more than a thousand less fortunate people living in the encampments as well. A meter in front of me was an elderly woman in a man's long woolen coat who had dug herself a hole in the mud in what I could only assume was an attempt to get warm, but her eyes were closed and she shivered. A toothless man sat on a paint can, holding a dirty blanket around his shoulders, looking utterly forlorn. Several kids our age sat in a circle around a small fire, their hands outstretched for warmth. We approached them.

"Why are all these people camped out around the Tractorstroy?" I asked.

The boy smirked. "We call it Tractorzloy."

"You call it the tractor lie instead of the tractor works?" asked Slavko.

"Yes," said the boy. "Because here, the tractors don't work."

"How about all these people?" I asked, gesturing with my arms to indicate the people camped out in the fields around the factory. "Do they have work here?"

"They only hire people from the city, or foreigners," he said.

"Then why are all these people staying?" asked Slavko.

The boy opened his mouth to say something but one of his friends punched him in the shoulder. "Ostap, don't talk to strangers," said the friend.

Ostap frowned at his friend. "I'll tell them if I want to, Ruslan," he said. Then he turned to Slavko and said, "Sometimes we can get odd jobs and we're paid in food."

"Thanks for telling us," Slavko responded.

As we continued through the encampment, we passed a number of tractors that seemed to have been discarded in the mud and scrubland. At one of them, a woman had attached an oilcloth tarp to the top of it and staked the bottom of the cloth into the ground, fashioning a half tent for herself. The woman looked up at us and smiled as we passed, so we paused for a moment to chat with her.

"Won't you get into trouble for using a tractor as a tent?" I asked her.

"Why would they care what I did with a tractor that doesn't work?"

"What about the other tractors out here?" asked Slavko, pointing to one that was flipped on its side. "Do they work?"

"None of them work," she said.

No wonder the place was now sarcastically being called Tractorzloy!

We continued through the encampment until we got to the other side of it, then stepped onto the road that bordered the apartment complex. We followed the road to the front of the apartment complex and kept on walking until we got to the front of the factory. The entrance itself looked imposing, with columns of bricks and windows framing large double doors. The brick wall that we helped to build extended from both sides of the entrance and wrapped all the way around the factory portion of the complex. The wall would have looked impressive had it not been slapped together so haphazardly. Back when we were making it, the leaders were so anxious for us to finish it that they rewarded speed over precision. Uneven mortar had hardened sloppily between the bricks. The courtyard area in front of the entrance was paved for cars and foot traffic, and the railway track had freight cars stacked with finished tractors. Two guards paced in front of the entrance.

"Do you think those boys were telling us the truth?" asked Slavko.

"About not hiring farmers?" I asked. "Maybe. But why don't we find out for ourselves?"

"Good idea," said Slavko.

We walked up to the closest guard, but when we were a couple of meters away, he turned and raised his gun at us. "Don't come any closer," he said.

"Greetings, Comrade," I said in the most cordial tone that I could muster. "We would like to apply for a job at the tractor plant."

The guard looked us up and down. "You're kulaks," he said. "Get lost."

"What is required to apply for a job?" I asked.

"You need your identification papers," he said. "But even with those, it's hard to get hired here. There are ten people waiting in line for every job at the plant."

We turned and left.

"What should we do now?" I asked Slavko. "If we can't get a job, we won't be able to get any more food, let alone save money to get to Ternopil."

"I don't feel good," said Slavko.

He looked like he was about ready to fall. We'd had nothing to eat since that bite of salo.

"Let's sit for a bit," I said.

I chose a spot at the edge of the walkway where it was dry. Slavko sat down beside me.

"Can we each have a small bite of salo?" he whispered.

I looked around. There were no encampments at the front of the tractor plant, and there were no people milling about. I took the package out of my pocket and folded down the paper from part of it. "Be quick," I said.

Slavko put his hands over mine and bit into the corner of the salo. Just as I was holding it up to my own lips, someone kicked me hard in the ribs. The salo was snatched out of my hands.

Ostap's friend Ruslan had snatched it from me and ran down the road. I jumped up from the ground. My ribs throbbed from the kick. I took off after him. He was quite a way ahead of me, but he turned to look and wasn't watching where he was going. He stepped right into a pothole and fell.

I caught up with him and sat on his back so he couldn't get up. He fought and flailed, but I finally wrested the salo from his hands. He had been running with the package opened and when he fell it had landed in the mud. It was squished and dirty, but I shoved it deep into my pocket. Slavko had caught up to us, and he stood beside me, his hands clenched in fists.

"What a thief you are," he said to Ruslan.

"Serves you right for eating food in front of people," said Ruslan, walking away with an indignant look on his face.

Once he was gone, I said to Slavko, "We've got to be more careful."

"I don't know where we can eat without being watched," said Slavko. "This place is swarming with hungry people."

"Just stand there and keep an eye out for a minute," I said. And then I reached into my pocket and pinched off a corner of the dirty salo. I popped it into my mouth, grit and all, then without taking the package out of my pocket, I folded the paper back around it the best that I could. This bit of salo was as precious as gold.

While chasing Ruslan, we had ended up running the entire length of the tractor complex. We now stood in front of the massive complex of workers' barracks. A worker came out of one of the buildings and noticed us standing there.

"You, kulaks, get away from here!" he said.

"We're not doing anything," said Slavko.

"Get out of here now," shouted the man, raising his hand to hit us.

"Come on," I said to Slavko. "Let's go."

We ended up walking all the way back to the encampment in the scrubland across from the apartment complex, and by the time we got there, I was utterly exhausted.

CHAPTER EIGHTEEN
TRACTORZLOY

An old man and woman with a kid my age were sitting around a small fire, warming a pot of something that smelled vile. There were other people camped out in various parts of the ravine as well. After the nasty treatment we'd received from just about everybody since we got here, I chose a spot as far from everyone else as I could. It was on the walkway and gave us a good view of one of the apartment buildings.

"Wouldn't it be funny if Alice and her father lived in there?" I asked Slavko as I spread my coat down on the ground.

We sat side by side and watched the people going in and out of the building. Slavko leaned against me, and I put my arm around his shoulder. I had no idea how we were going to get to Ternopil, but right now I just wanted to go to sleep. But how could we possibly find a place that was safe for the night?

The people who went in and out of the apartment buildings looked more prosperous than anyone else we had seen since we got here. They were clean and they looked healthy and no one shouted at us to leave. I felt my eyes get heavy, and I nearly fell asleep. But then a hand landed on my shoulder, and I jerked awake.

"You need to get out of here right now," said an unfamiliar voice behind me.

I turned around. It was the kid who had been with the couple cooking something vile. Except the couple was no longer there. "Why?" I asked.

"Look over there," he said.

Uniformed men were pulling people from the encampment and loading them into the back of a truck.

"Come on." He pointed to the buildings at the far end of the complex, farthest from the main road.

As we trotted behind the boy, the farmers in the encampment fled. The boy darted down a walkway between two buildings at the back of the complex. I lost sight of him for a moment, but then heard a low whistle. He gestured for us to climb through a main-floor window.

Once we were inside, the boy closed the window and pulled the curtains.

It took a minute or so for my heart to stop pounding and my eyes to adjust to the dimness of the room. The floors were streaked with mud and the walls were cobwebbed, but there was a wooden table with chairs around it, so I sat down on one of them. Slavko and the boy did the same.

"Thank you for helping us," I said to the boy. "I'm Nyl. This is my brother, Slavko."

"I'm Ihor," said the boy.

"Where did your parents go?" I asked.

"Parents?" he asked. "You mean the people with the cook pot? They're no relation. I had fish bones and they had a pot, so we made a deal and shared some fish soup."

"How did you get fish bones?" I asked.

"The foreign specialists who live in these buildings will sometimes pay you with food scraps if you do jobs for them."

"Oh," I said. "Another kid mentioned something similar."

"How come there's no one living in this flat?" asked Slavko.

"There's a lot broken in this flat, and none of the foreigners want to live in it," said Ihor. "I will be sleeping in here tonight. You can too if you want, but we've got to be gone first thing in the morning. The police are constantly trying to clear us out."

It wasn't just us and Ihor who slept there that night, it was Ostap and Ruslan as well. Ruslan looked as surprised as I felt when he dropped down through the window.

"You've got to stop taking advantage of new people," said Ihor, punching Ruslan in the shoulder. "I saw you try to steal from Nyl. The way you act, it's no better than the shock workers."

"Look, I'm sorry," said Ruslan, holding out a hand to shake mine. "But when you passed us, I could smell that smoked salo. It was driving me crazy with hunger."

"Here's how it works," said Ihor. He reached into his pocket and pulled out a hunk of black bread. "This goes on the table for us all to share. Now you, Ruslan."

Ruslan reached inside his coat sleeve and drew out a raw potato. He set it down on the table. Ostap set down another piece of black bread. All eyes were on me. I looked over to Slavko. He gave a slight nod. I reached into my pocket and drew out our mashed-up and dirty package of salo and set it on the table. "This is my brother's and my contribution," I said.

"This is a feast," said Ihor.

The apartment didn't have lights or heat, but it did have a water tap. One of the boys found an old, empty tin can, so we twisted off the lid. The can made a perfect drinking cup, and the lid was useful as a knife to divide up the bread and potato, and we sliced the salo with it too. After we had eaten, the boys told us how they survived day by day at the tractor factory.

"The best way to get food is by collecting firewood," said Ruslan.

"Why do they need firewood?" I asked.

"The apartments have coal furnaces, but there's never enough coal," said Ostap. "So wood is better than nothing."

"How can I get identification papers?" asked Slavko. "I want to work in the plant."

"Impossible," said Ihor. "Farmers are banned from working here."

"But how do they even know where someone is from?" asked Slavko.

"Each person is thoroughly investigated before they're hired," said Ihor. "If they pass and they get hired, they're issued an identification card with their photograph on it. They can't get past the guards unless they show that card. Even if someone worked here for a long time but lost their card, they would be out of luck. They'd lose their job."

Slavko looked crestfallen at this news. "I really wanted to work at the plant," he said.

"Remember, this is Tractorzloy. Nothing works. You would have been disappointed even if you managed to get hired," said Ihor.

Slavko and I hung around with the other boys as much as we could because they knew how to evade the police and also knew the best spots beyond the ravine for gathering firewood. Each night we'd find a place to sleep, but at the beginning it was rarely in the same place two nights in a row. After a while, Slavko and I settled on sleeping in the communal laundry building. The reason? It was heated, for one thing, and we had as much water as we wanted. But also, it was easy to hide from the police in there. When anyone opened the door, it made a screeching noise, and that gave us plenty of time to hide.

Slavko continued selling firewood, but eventually I got some of the foreign specialists to pay me to do their laundry. I convinced them to pay us a bit extra for staying in the laundry building overnight. One of the engineers was so happy to have me do his laundry that he bribed the police to let us stay there so we could protect his drying laundry from theft.

In Felivka, laundry was hand scrubbed on big wooden racks down by the river in the summer and in a washtub in the kitchen in the winter. There was no river to wash in at the tractor plant, which was why they needed a laundry building. Inside were washtubs with scrubbing racks and brushes, rinse tubs, and clotheslines. I would scrub clothing, towels, and sheets on the racks with a bar of soap, then wring each item out by hand, transfer it to the rinse tub to soak while the next load was in the washtub. It took strength and dexterity to wring the water out of the larger items like bedsheets, and it was awkward hanging them on the line by myself. But word got around that I did a good job. Slavko would pick up the laundry when he delivered his firewood, and he'd deliver the cleaned laundry on his route. We each got paid mostly in small pieces of black bread.

I desperately wanted to be paid in money so we could at least travel part of the way to Ternopil by train, but money was scarce, and so was food, so we took what they gave us. We were hungry and cold most of the time, but having access to the laundry meant we stayed cleaner and healthier than just about any of the other farmers.

Almost every day, I witnessed someone die. Once it was a regular factory worker walking back to the barracks after his shift. His knees crumpled and he fell to the ground, dead. I was shocked that someone who had a salary and a place to live could still starve to death, but the regular workers weren't paid enough to buy much food. They had to rely on the company cafeteria, which I was told meant a piece of black bread and maybe a bowl of broth during a sixteen-hour workday. The specialists were paid far more than that, and as far as I could see, they weren't starving, but they were hungry.

Another time, it was a kid who died. He'd just come in from the country, so we had him stay with us that night. But he stayed curled on the floor when the rest of us got up in the morning. His death was so very similar to the way Tato had died that it hit me hard. I comforted myself with the thought that he wasn't alone when he died and his stomach hadn't been empty. His last night on earth had been spent with homeless kids just like himself, sharing food and stories and friendship.

Trucks came around each evening to pick up the dead bodies. I thought of the pit where they dumped the dead in Felivka since the hunger began. The tractor plant complex was so huge compared to our village and so many more deaths occurred each day. Were these unfortunates thrown into a garbage pit like Tato had been? I shuddered to think of how big the pit for Tractorzloy must be.

"We're better off here than we were in Felivka," said Slavko one day as he helped me soap down shirts. "Why don't we just stay here?"

"Doing hard labor and being paid in moldy bread while people die of starvation around us?" I asked. "What kind of life is that? We need to get to Ternopil."

"Like Mama said, we may as well try for the moon," said Slavko. "Getting to Ternopil is just as impossible."

"We can do it one step at a time," I said. "Our first step was to get out of Felivka alive. We did that. Next step is to get to Kharkiv. We can find Roman."

"What makes you think Roman knows how to get to Ternopil?" asked Slavko.

"Maybe he doesn't," I said. "But he can help us survive in Kharkiv until we find that out for ourselves."

Slavko didn't respond, but he pounded the next shirt with extra vigor. Finally he said, "It bothers me that we're right here at the tractor plant but we can't work in the tractor plant. We haven't even been inside."

"You know that it's carefully guarded," I said. "Let's concentrate on getting to Kharkiv in one piece."

CHAPTER NINETEEN
USEFUL FOOLS

Slavko was out collecting firewood while I was busy in the laundry, scrubbing out a particularly difficult oil stain from a cotton shirt. The door creaked open. I looked up, expecting to see my brother coming back early.

But it was Alice.

She carried a basket of clothing in her arms. I set my bar of soap onto the side of the scrubbing rack and stood so she could see me.

"Is that you, Alice?" I called out.

She lowered her laundry basket and looked at me. Her jaw dropped. "Nyl from Felivka? What are you doing here?"

"I've been here for a while, my brother Slavko too. I've been looking for you, but this is a big place."

"Why did you want to find me?" she asked.

"I wanted to let you know that all the things you and your father told us turned out to be lies."

"What do you mean?" she asked.

"Comrade White said the kolkhoz would get tractors and modern equipment for farming. They didn't send enough tractors, and those they did send broke down. He said everyone's life would be better, but many in our village have been killed, starved to death, or deported. He promised we'd be able to grow more grain. That's the biggest lie of all. They took our horses and our seeds. We can't grow grain at all."

Her face went bright pink. "You're blaming this all on us? Papa and I were only doing what we thought was right."

"Maybe you should think before you act," I said.

Alice dropped her basket onto the floor. The laundry spilled all over the place. She turned and fled out the door.

I was so angry with myself. She and her father had been tricked into helping Stalin. They weren't bad people, just mistaken. Even so, their actions had caused a lot of damage. I ran out and caught up with her.

"Go away," she said.

"I'm sorry," I said. "But seeing you made me so angry. We've lost everything because of Stalin's useful fools. My parents are dead, Yulia betrayed us, and now we have no place to live."

She stopped and turned. "Your parents are dead?"

I took a deep breath. "Yes."

"Because of the shock workers?"

"Yes."

"And what's this about Yulia?"

A sob caught in my throat. I took a deep breath to calm myself, then said, "She told Chort about a small amount of grain we had kept so we wouldn't starve. Chort confiscated it, and he beat Tato so severely that it eventually killed him. Sometime after that, Chort shot our mother."

Alice looked stricken. For a long moment she said nothing and then a tear trickled down one of her cheeks. "I'm sorry," she said. "We should never have come here. They lied to us as well."

"You and your father weren't controlling anything," I said. "I know that. It's just that everything started to go bad when you arrived in our village."

She stood there with her head bowed. "I wish there was something that I could do to help you."

"Maybe there is," I said. "I want to get Slavko and me out of the Soviet Union. Maybe you and your father could help us."

She looked up. "Papa and I want to get out too."

"Would you and your father consider helping us?" I asked.

"I gladly would," she said. "Probably Papa too. Let me think about this."

"Let's get that laundry off the floor," I said.

She turned and we walked back toward the laundry building together.

We gathered her clothing items in silence and put them back into the hamper. And she grabbed a big wash-basin to start the tedious procedure of sorting, wetting, sudsing, scrubbing, rinsing, wringing, and hanging the clothing to dry.

She paused midscrub, then looked over to me. "Can you come back to the apartment with me when we're done here? That way we could both speak to Papa about it together."

CHAPTER TWENTY
PASSPORTS

Slavko joined us in the laundry when he finished his last firewood delivery, so he came with us to Alice's flat. Their unit was on the top floor of the last building at the back of the complex. They had one room and a bathroom for the two of them. The room was set up with two mattresses on the floor, and they were sectioned off from each other with a clothesline with shirts and pants and skirts draped over it. Beside each mattress a suitcase sat near the pillow as a sort of night table. On one of them was a well-thumbed copy of *The Communist Manifesto*. On the other, a framed photograph of an older woman with short, curled hair.

"Is that your grandmother?" I asked.

"Yes." Alice picked up the photograph and handed it to me so I could get a better look.

"She has kind eyes," I said.

"I love her so much," said Alice. "And she misses me terribly."

The comment twisted my heart. I had been so focused on my own troubles that I hadn't bothered to think of all the sacrifices that Alice had made. She and her father had come here with good intentions but they were duped into helping with Stalin's murderous plans. I was still angry with her, but I had some sympathy too.

"Have you had letters from her?" I asked.

"We write to each other," she said. "But I have to be careful about how much I tell her. The letters are censored. Sometimes the ones I receive have black marks through them, so I can only imagine what mine look like by the time they get to Toronto."

I set the photograph back down on the suitcase.

There was a table with chairs at the opposite end of the room, and in the corner near the sitting area was the obligatory atheist's corner. Theirs featured a giant poster of Lenin affixed to the wall above the usual portrait of Stalin in a wooden frame on the table. The bathroom had a flush toilet, a sink, and a shower.

Slavko sat at the table, and Alice looked out the big window in front of the balcony. I stepped up beside her and looked at homeless encampments spread out as far as the eye could see.

"No one told us it would be like this," she said, making a sweeping motion with her hand to indicate all the unfortunates who had been stripped of food and home after being labeled kulaks and who were now living in the most desperate circumstances imaginable.

"What was it like in Canada?" I asked.

"Not perfect, if that's what you're asking," she said. "We're in the middle of an economic depression. But at least the government isn't stealing food from starving people."

Just then, Comrade White walked in. His eyes darted from Slavko to me, and then to his daughter. "This is a surprise," he said.

"Their parents have been killed," said Alice in a quiet voice. "And it's our fault. I think we should help them escape the Soviet Union."

Comrade White's eyes widened at his daughter's words. "That's a lot to take in all at once," he said, sitting down beside Slavko.

"We'll tell you all about it," I said.

We talked for hours, telling Comrade White and Alice about the terrible things that continued to happen in our village and all that we had seen on our way through the countryside.

"The same is happening here," said Comrade White. "Stalin does not value the life of his people. The regular factory workers are being starved and worked to death while foreigners like us are given better food and more of it to bribe us into keeping quiet."

"I was shocked to see how hungry and exhausted the regular factory workers look," I said.

"Their weekly pay isn't enough to buy even one meal." Comrade White threw up his hands in exasperation. "And the slop they're fed at the factory is all they have to live on."

"Compared to us, they're fortunate," said Slavko.

Comrade White sighed. "Did you know that there are seventeen levels of worthiness here? The higher the level, the more food you get. And guess who's at the bottom?" He pointed first to me and then to Slavko. "The people who grow the food."

"I bet I can guess who's at the top," I said. "The shock workers."

"At the very top are the Communist Party bosses. Foreign journalists are given all sorts of riches as bribery to write lies about Stalin's five-year plan. I want to get back home so I can tell people the truth. It would be important for you and your brother to get out as well, not just for yourselves, but as witnesses to what's happening here." He got up from the table and began to pace.

"Does that mean you'll help us to get out of the Soviet Union?" I asked.

"Yes," he said. "But let me think this through. You can't look like kulaks, and you need identification papers."

"We'll need to get our own passports back from Kovalev," Alice said to her father.

"You're right," said Comrade White. "We've got our Soviet papers, but Kovalev, the head Communist at the factory, put our Canadian passports into the safe."

We met up again a week later at the Whites' flat. They had saved some of their food rations over the week and shared it with us. There was coarse brown bread that was much easier to chew than the black bread we were given in payment for chores, plus there was a small piece of some sort of meat and a boiled potato for each of us. I had to be careful not to wolf it down because my stomach wasn't used to so much food.

"We've been thinking things through," said Alice. "Even though we're not considered kulaks, our movement is also watched. Papa can't get our passports from Kovalev."

"Why not?" I asked.

"Turns out, even asking for them would trigger an interrogation," said Comrade White. "We'll only be able to use our Soviet identification."

"We don't even have that," I said. "It's going to be a challenge even getting into Kharkiv, let alone Ternopil. Ihor told me the police arrest farmers who try to get into any of the cities."

"That's true," said Alice. "But wait until you see what Papa has for you."

Comrade White reached into his shirt pocket and pulled out two documents. He set them on the table.

I reached for one and opened it. A Soviet identification paper. The boy looked to be close to my age and his hair was dark like mine. He was a Young Pioneer from Kharkiv. I slid it across the table so Slavko could look at it, then opened the second one. Another boy. Similar age and coloring, also from Kharkiv, also a Young Pioneer.

"Where did you get these?" I asked.

"Both boys died working at the tractor factory, and I have been quietly collecting items like this so they can be used to help other victims."

"They're not our photos or our names," said Slavko.

"I know," said Comrade White. "But I can take your photographs with my camera and replace their names and pictures with yours. Now you two are just going to have to figure out how to look like city people."

CHAPTER TWENTY-ONE
DIED OF EATING

July 1932

Slavko sat across from me as I was roasting a potato over a fire when I heard a familiar voice behind me say, "Well, if it isn't Nyl and Slavko from Felivka."

I turned around. It was Lev. "Hello, old friend," I said.

He pulled a potato out of his own pocket and held it up. "Mind if we share the fire?"

"Take a seat," said Slavko, making space on the rusted tractor wheel that he had been using as a chair.

"Is Petro here with you?" I asked.

"He's bringing some firewood," he said.

Petro appeared a few minutes later and added some twigs to the flames. He plopped down cross-legged on the ground. "When did you two get back here?" he asked.

"We've been here since late March," said Slavko. "What about you?"

"We went home, but then came back almost immediately," said Petro. "Mama died of eating, so we had no family left."

"She died of eating?" I asked.

Petro sighed. He opened his mouth to speak, but the words wouldn't come out. Lev got up and knelt beside him, placing a hand on his brother's shoulder. "Do you want me to tell them about it?" he asked.

Petro nodded.

"Mama started to hallucinate from lack of food. She carved the raw flesh from a rotted cow and ate it," he said. "She was that crazed with hunger. The local shock worker laughed as he told us about her painful final hours."

I held my head in my hands and closed my eyes in sorrow. My heart went out to Lev and Petro, and to their mother. "Vichnaya pamyat," I whispered.

"Vichnaya pamyat," Lev, Petro, and Slavko whispered back.

As we sat there in silence for long minutes, I watched the flames lick the wood. I broke the silence by saying, "We're getting out of here. You can come with us, if you want."

"Getting out of where?" asked Lev.

"The Soviet Union," I said. And I told him about our plan.

"We've got our papers too," he said. "Pickpocketed from corpses. But I think we'll stay here."

"Why would you want to stay here?" I asked. "This place is like one huge graveyard of rotted dreams."

"Ever since we organized our forged papers, we've been on the waiting list for a spot in the tractor plant," said Lev. "I'm fairly high up on the list now, what with all the deaths. If I got in there, I'd get fed every day, and I'd be able to share my bunk in the barracks with Petro."

"Don't you want more out of life than one bite of food a day and half a bed?"

"Like what?" asked Petro. "When you haven't had meals or a place to sleep for as long as us, it sounds pretty good."

The brothers' reasoning made me sad. I didn't want to be just a cog in Stalin's evil machine. I wanted to live in a world where people were equal no matter who their parents were or where they were born. I wanted to live in a place where hard work and kindness were valued. Was that too much to ask for? I didn't argue with Lev and Petro though. They also deserved the right to choose their own life.

That week, Slavko and I worked on changing our appearance. I hated the idea of stealing, but the laundry provided me with the perfect opportunity for transformation. I was careful to spread my pilfering around so that I only took one item from any given family, but I managed to get a nice shirt and pants for me and also a set for Slavko. Since it was midsummer, we had no need of coats, which was a good thing, since no one asked me to wash their coats.

The week before we were to leave, it was time for our photos. Comrade White invited Slavko and me to their flat so we could each have a thorough shower and wash our hair. When we were finished, Alice gave us each a haircut.

"I've been cutting Papa's hair for years," she explained. "My grandmother is a hairdresser, and she taught me how to do this."

"I've been cutting my own hair for years," I said. "And nobody taught me how."

"That explains why it's such a mess," she said.

Her comment annoyed me, but when I looked into the mirror after she had finished my haircut, I was surprised at how different I looked. When I cut it myself, my goal was just to keep it out of my face, but Alice had managed to shape it so there were no chunks sticking out anywhere. I didn't want to admit it, but she'd done a good job.

I felt like a new person, smelling like soap, my head light from the haircut, and looking stylish in the city clothing. I hardly recognized Slavko. His getup made him look much more mature, which was a good thing, seeing as his passport would list him as the same age as me.

Alice gave us each a red tie so we could look like Young Pioneers, but after Comrade White took our photos I stuck mine in my pocket. There were lots of real Young Pioneers here at the tractor plant and especially among the kids of the specialists. They might have recognized right away that I was a phony. Alice also found a satchel with a shoulder strap for Slavko and a small shoulder bag for me. "This makes it look like you've got a home and like you're just out for the day," she said. "That should help set you apart from the kulaks as well."

I would have loved to put something I cherished inside my shoulder bag, but I had nothing. Alice must have had an inkling about my thoughts, because she went into her bedroom and came back with a few things. "Here," she said, handing me a pencil and paper and a set of playing cards. "Now it looks like your case has a purpose."

Waiting for our papers to be doctored was one of the longest weeks of my life, but Slavko and I were both excited to hold the counterfeit documents in our hands.

The next morning we would be leaving. I could hardly contain my excitement.

CHAPTER TWENTY-TWO
BETRAYED

"I'm staying at Tractorgavod," said Slavko. He planned the timing of his announcement with care. We had gotten up and dressed and were supposed to be meeting Comrade White and Alice in front of their building in an hour.

"You mean Tractorzloy," I said in a low controlled voice even though I felt like shouting.

"You know that working at Tractorgavod is all I've ever wanted to do," he said. "You're the one who wants to go to Ternopil, not me. And I'm not stopping you."

"But you're my brother. My only family. We should stay together."

"There's still Yulia," he said. "We're family too, and this way I'll stay close to her."

"I don't think I can ever forgive her for betraying our family the way that she did."

"I'm trying to forgive her," said Slavko. "And I hope you will forgive me."

"What do you think you're going to do here?" I asked. "Gather firewood for foreigners all your life?"

"I've applied to the factory," he said. "I'm all cleaned up, and I have my identity papers. Lev took me to the office, and I've already had my interview. I passed."

"You've got a job already?"

"No," he said. "But I'm on the waiting list. Even if it takes a year, it's what I want to do."

"You'll work sixteen-hour days and get paid practically nothing. Is that what you want?"

"If it means I get to work with tractors, yes."

I felt like punching something, but instead I just paced. I took a deep breath, forcing myself to calm down. "Will you write to me?" I asked.

"Nyl, of course I will," said Slavko, his eyes filling with tears. "You're my big brother."

I took out the paper and pencil that Alice had given me and wrote down the address of Auntie Pawlina's cousins, then handed it to him. "We're not going to be there for quite some time," I said. "But it would be wonderful if there was a letter from my little brother waiting for me when I got there."

"There will be," said Slavko. "And thank you for not being too angry."

I gave him a fierce hug.

Alice stood at the entrance of her apartment building,

chatting with the driver of a hired horse and wagon. Her father was nowhere in sight.

"Good morning, Comrade Alice," I said, making myself look as calm as I could. "Are you looking forward to seeing the Derzhprom?" This had been our story, that three student friends were being taken on a day trip by Comrade White to Kharkiv to see the Derzhprom, Stalin's pride of Soviet architecture. That would be less suspicious than having us dropped off at the Kharkiv train station. Except where was Comrade White? And of course now there was no Slavko either.

"I am looking forward to the day," she said, a smile pasted onto her face. "But I forgot something upstairs. Can you come up with me?"

"I would be happy to."

"Don't be long," said the driver. "I've got another fare after I drop you off."

"We'll just be a minute," said Alice.

Once we were on the stairwell, I was going to ask Alice where her father was, but she held a finger to her lips. I followed her in silence up the stairs, down the hall-way, and into her apartment.

The place had been torn apart, and her father was nowhere in sight.

"What happened . . . ?"

She grabbed my arm and pulled me close, then whispered into my ear, "He's been arrested. Where's your brother?"

"He's decided to stay here," I whispered.

She smashed the portrait of Stalin and shook the shards of glass onto her mattress, then tore at the painting until the top of Stalin's head was in shreds. She drew a small packet out from behind and opened it up. She groaned. It was empty. She muttered something under her breath and threw the packet on the floor.

"One more spot to check. Come on."

I followed her out the door and down the hallway. She stopped in front of one of her neighbor's doors and pointed to a vent in the ceiling.

"Can you boost me up?" she asked.

I crouched. "Hop on my back." Her hard shoes balanced on my shoulder blades as I tried to keep still so she wouldn't fall.

"Got it," she said, hopping off my back.

She handed me a thick envelope and I stuffed it into my bag.

"Weren't there supposed to be four of you?" asked the driver when we got into the wagon.

"The others have gone on ahead," said Alice. "We'll meet them at the Derzhprom."

"Suit yourself," said the driver. "But Comrade White paid me for four people and I'm keeping it all."

"That's fine," said Alice.

As the horse began to trot away, my heart ached with the thought of leaving my brother behind. I scanned the clusters of escaped farmers in the encampments as we passed by them, looking for a last glimpse of Slavko, but I didn't see him.

Soon, we turned onto the road and Tractorzloy was behind us.

Ragged, bone-weary people, walking in ones and twos, trudged along the side of the road, and our driver casually maneuvered around them. More than once he had to dodge a person lying on the road, either dead or in the last gasps of life, and my heart lurched with sadness each time. Did their families know the fate of their loved one? Or maybe they were the last of their family. That made me think of Slavko, now on his own at the factory, without me there to protect him. Should I have stayed? I had one brother and one sister. We were all alive still, yet not together. That didn't seem right. But Slavko made his own decision about how and where he would live. I wasn't angry about his decision, but it worried me a lot. I was desperate to keep him safe. Yulia was a different matter.

I tried to take my mind off Slavko by looking out at the landscape. It was midsummer, near harvest time, and on both sides of us were fields that should have been lush with wheat, but weeds were choking the wheat. It would be a poor crop for another year. This rich black earth should have been bursting with life, but if you take away the farmers, their seeds, their horses, and their food, what do you expect? Did Stalin think the wheat would plant and harvest itself?

The sight of all this waste filled me with dread. What would it take for Stalin to realize that it was his policies, not his so-called kulaks, who were the enemy of the people?

The landscape began to change, with fields giving way to buildings; up ahead of us, the horizon showed more buildings. We were entering the great city of Kharkiv.

We approached a wide, flat river and our road went over a bridge that was manned by police. Our driver paused, and one of the officers stepped over to our wagon. "Identification papers, comrades," he said to us, holding out his hand. I pulled out my forged document and put it in his palm, hoping that he wouldn't notice the trembling of my hand. He glanced at me with bored eyes, then scanned my paper. He handed it back. I guess my haircut and clean clothing made me look like I was from the city.

The officer spent more time on Alice's papers. "You're from Canada?"

"I am, Comrade," she said.

"How do you like it here?" he asked.

"I love it," she said, her teeth clenched into a smile.

"Not surprising," he said. "It's paradise for the common man here." He handed back her papers, then walked away.

A feeling of relief coursed through me as our wagon continued down a long, flat residential street that bordered the river. I knew we still had a lot of challenges ahead of us, but at least my papers hadn't raised suspicion. We'd got into the first big city and past the police. I hardly noticed the buildings and the people on the streets. I was desperate to talk to Alice, to find out what happened to her father, and to tell her about Slavko's decision.

Finally the driver pulled up to a street corner and turned to Alice. "We're here."

"Thank you," said Alice as we both got out of the wagon.

All at once, I took in our surroundings. I had seen the Derzhprom in photographs and drawings, but it was a whole different experience to stand in front of this magnificent ring of modern buildings that seemed to reach the sky.

Alice and I walked through the circular courtyard until we got to an open space between two of the giant connected buildings. I looked up at the sleek glass-and-concrete walkway high above us. What would it feel like to step into that corridor suspended in the air? Was anyone up there now, looking down on us?

Just then, I heard whispers. I turned. Two children, maybe three or four years old, and a girl, maybe my age. They came out from behind a pile of construction trash.

Their clothing was shredded and dirty. No matter how many starved kids I encountered, I could never get used to them.

The older girl came up to me and put her hand on my sleeve. "Please, Comrade," she said. "Do you have any food at all? My sisters are starving."

I felt in my pockets. Miraculously, I still had a heel of hard black bread from last night's supper. I took it out and gave it to her.

"Thank you," she said, holding the stale bread up to her face and inhaling its scent. She slipped back into the shadows.

Alice stood there, watching. "Do you have any more bread?" she asked.

"I don't," I said.

"Money?"

"No."

"Neither do I. They took all our cash and our ration stamps when Papa was arrested. All I have is my Canadian birth certificate and my Soviet identification papers. Just keep in mind that we need to eat too."

"But how could I ignore that girl's plea?" I asked. "Did you see how young her sisters were?"

"I understand," she said. "But there are things you need to know."

She took my elbow and led me to the center of the vast open area in the middle of the ring of connected buildings.

I slowly turned to take in the entire complex. Each building was connected to the ones on either side with covered walkways on various floors. It reminded me a little bit of the beaded necklace Mama got from Tato as a wedding present, with the buildings being the amber beads and the walkways being the chain. "This is an amazing building," I said.

"We're in the middle of the city, but we're completely alone here," whispered Alice.

I looked around again and realized that she was right. No cars, no people on foot, now that the starving kids had disappeared. The area seemed almost abandoned. "This is a good place to talk," I said.

"Papa has been accused of being a spy," said Alice.

"Then why did we leave? We should have stayed to defend him," I said. "And maybe I should have stayed with my brother."

"No," said Alice. "If we stayed, they could have tortured me as a way of punishing Papa. If I'm gone, that takes away their biggest weapon. Besides, I need to get the photographs out."

"What photographs?" I asked.

"That envelope I gave you," she said. "It's filled with photographs of things that shocked Papa, like workers collapsing from hunger on the assembly line and starving farmers in the encampments around the factory being rounded up and beaten. He's been developing the pictures himself, using our bathroom as a dark room, but someone must have found out and denounced him. All along, we knew the risk we were taking, but Papa and I both wanted to do the right thing. We hid a few of the photographs in the flat, but they found those. Thankfully, we have these," she said, tapping my bag. "I need to get the pictures out."

"Out to where?" I asked.

"To the newspapers in America. Maybe if people saw with their own eyes what was happening here, there would be fewer useful fools like me and Papa coming all the way here to help Stalin. And if governments stopped buying Stalin's wheat, maybe he'd stop stealing it from people like you."

Alice's words hit me like a jolt of lightning. I couldn't bring my father or mother back to life. I couldn't change what Slavko or Yulia wanted to do, but I could help Alice escape so she could show the world Stalin's murders.

"I'll help you in any way I can."

"I was hoping you'd say that." She took a deep, shuddering breath and composed herself for a moment. Then she said, "Now tell me, why isn't Slavko with you?"

"He wants to get a job at the tractor plant."

"That's a terrible idea," said Alice.

"I hope he'll realize that before it's too late. Right now, you and I have to figure out how to get out of here."

"Maybe there's a way of sneaking onto the train," said Alice.

CHAPTER TWENTY-THREE
JUST ALICE

Alice had lived in Kharkiv before Tractorzloy was finished, and so she knew how to get around. The train station was quite a distance from the Derzhprom, which meant that I got a better sense of the city as we walked away from the quiet emptiness of the Derzhprom complex. Within a few blocks, we stepped into a market area with a state store, a commercial store, and a Torgsin store. All of them had signs for food, and each had a long line outside.

"If we had ration stamps and money, we could buy food at the state store," said Alice. "That's where I always shopped when we lived in Kharkiv. It's the cheapest, but it's only for party members."

"What about the commercial store?" I asked.

"If you run out of ration stamps, you have to buy food from there, but it's really expensive."

"And the Torgsin?"

"The most expensive. They sell fancy food," said Alice. "Like chocolates and caviar. They don't accept rubles, only things like gold, jewels, and foreign money."

Most of the people in the Torgsin line looked like shock workers, government officials, and foreigners, but there was also a hungry woman in a dusty country dress, her hand resting on the shoulder of a bone-thin boy who leaned into her.

I stepped over to the woman. "Greetings, Pani," I said. "Maybe you should try the commercial store. This one is very expensive."

"I'm a farmer," said the woman. "I have no rubles. I'm selling this." She opened her palm and showed me two plain gold wedding rings. "I'm too thin now, and mine keeps falling off. My husband died of hunger. The other ring was his. I'm hoping they'll give me a loaf of bread for these so my son can live for a few more days."

"Not likely," said a man standing behind her. "My guess is half a loaf."

"People from the country aren't allowed to buy in the other stores?" I asked Alice as we walked away.

"She might be able to buy at the commercial store if she had Soviet cash," said Alice. "But the government is trying to discourage farmers from flooding into the cities."

"But they're starving people out of the villages. Are they all supposed to just stay where they are and die?"

"I know," said Alice. "It's terrible. And the Torgsin stores are another devious plan."

"What do you mean?"

"They cater to foreigners and high-ranking Communists, but they'll take gold from farmers. Stalin thinks farmers have lots of gold hidden, just like he thinks they have lots of grain hidden. He figures the Torgsin stores are a way of squeezing out their last bits of gold before they starve."

Alice's words made me furious but I realized that she spoke the truth. As we walked, we passed more people in the Torgsin line, and there were many desperate farmers like that woman and her child. They were mixed in with well-to-do foreigners and Communist bosses looking for treats. The farmers clutched golden icons that had probably been in their family for generations, crosses on chains, and wedding rings. And what would they get for them? A bit of bread and a few days more to live.

A woman in a black dress with a white lace apron on top of it was the first in line, and I wondered if she had been a farmer but was now the servant of one of the privileged. She waited a meter or so from the locked entrance to the store. Alice and I paused to watch.

The door opened, and a woman in a fancy dress walked out. The woman in black stepped in.

The one who came out was carrying a wicker basket, and the scent of smoky garlic wafted around her as she walked in front of us. I peered inside her basket. A link of kobasa, a small ham, apples, onions, and a loaf of rye bread. I'm not usually a thief, but we had to get food, and even if I stole all that this woman had, she wouldn't starve. I grabbed the kobasa.

The woman slapped my hand with such force that the kobasa fell onto the cobblestones and a couple of other items from her basket scattered onto the ground as well. Several people ran over and scrabbled for them.

"Let me help you with that," said Alice, throwing in some English words as well, but I couldn't understand them.

The woman seemed to be relieved that Alice was helping her, and they chatted away in English as Alice picked up the items from the ground. I didn't think the woman realized that Alice slipped something into her own pocket. Alice stood up and brushed off her hands, then she looked at me with a theatrical scowl and said in Ukrainian, "You should apologize to this fine lady so she doesn't call the police on you."

I clasped my hands in front of my chest and bowed to the woman. "My apologies," I said.

I walked away, and Alice walked away as if she didn't know me until we were out of the woman's sight.

Once we were out of the market area, I caught up to her and whispered, "What did you get?"

"Not much," she said. "I had to put back all the big stuff because she would have noticed that, but there were candies at the bottom of the basket. I grabbed some of those."

She handed me one. It was hard and square and wrapped in colorful waxy paper. I unwrapped it. "What is it, do you know?"

"Maybe toffee," she said. "Try it."

I popped it into my mouth and nearly swooned at the burst of sugar. "Mmmmm" was all I could say.

"What's on the paper?" asked Alice.

I unfolded the wrapping to reveal a sketch of a well-fed comrade navigating a tractor through a lush field of wheat. Did anyone think that's what the countryside looked like? Or maybe the people who could afford these candies were living in a fantasy world about what Stalin was up to.

Alice unwrapped a toffee for herself and popped it into her mouth as well. The look on her face was pure joy. She opened up her toffee paper and blanched. She was going to shove it into her pocket without showing me, but I grabbed it from her. It was supposed to be funny, but it wasn't. It was a cartoon of church bells being taken down and made into tractors, while a horrified kulak looked on. The comic hit too close to home and reminded me of how Alice and I first met.

My hunk of sweet toffee seemed to lodge into my throat. I sat down on the cobblestones and held my head in my hands. All this death and destruction—was it just a joke to Stalin and his collaborators?

Alice knelt beside me and put a hand on my arm. "I'm sorry that my actions ruined your life, but I'm trying to make it up to you. I'll get the pictures out," she said. "The world will know what's going on."

I raised my head and looked in her eyes. "But will anyone care?"

Her eyes flashed with anger.

"Get up," she said, pulling me to my feet. "Let's concentrate on what we can do to change the future instead of sitting around and complaining about what already happened."

But on our way to the train station, we passed desperate eyes of starving people from the countryside staring out at us from under steps, in corners, and as they lay huddled and listless in the street. How would getting the photographs out help these people? We also passed well-dressed, well-fed Communists who seemed oblivious to the hunger in front of them. I watched a woman step over a dead child as she licked a cone of ice cream. These people saw the starvation with their own eyes, yet they denied it. How would the photographs help? I was filled with feelings of anger and helplessness and frustration all wrapped together.

The Kharkiv train station was huge compared to the small wooden depot in Felivka. Starving children were lined up like sparrows, leaning against the side of the building, waiting to die or somehow escape. It was a repeat inside the station, with more desperate people hoping for one more day of life.

We looked at a map display of all the interconnecting train stations. "I don't know how we're going to manage this without tickets," Alice said, pointing out all the connections we'd need to make between Kharkiv and the station on the Soviet side that was closest to Ternopil. We'd have to walk after that. We'd have to figure out a way to cross the Zbruch River too. Was Auntie Pawlina there yet?

"The cheapest fare from Kharkiv to Kyiv is in rubles, not kopeks, and that's for just the first leg of the trip."

"Maybe we can sneak on a train," I said. "Let's check it out."

We went down the stairs to the platforms near the tracks. There was an old rusted train car that had been pulled off the track and left on its side, and children were huddled together in it. One of the boys saw me looking at him. He stuck out his tongue.

A train pulled in. Passengers pushed around us, and as they lined up to get on board, a guard holding a long stick came up to us and said, "Do you have tickets?"

"No," I said.

"Then get out of here before I arrest you."

We slowly turned and made to walk through the passage that led back into the station, but I wanted to see what those kids were up to. As the train began slowly chugging forward, one kid darted out from the rusted train car and ran onto the tracks, chasing it.

The guard saw him and shouted, "Get away from the train."

The boy grabbed on to the back of the train and pulled himself up. The guard ran up and whacked him with the stick. He fell off, smashing his head on the rail. More kids ran to the train. One leapt between two train cars, then hooted for joy. He must have made it. The guard knocked down one more kid and kept the others back. The train sped up and disappeared. Of all the kids who tried to get onto the train, only one made it. One lay injured, and the guard had two others by the scruff of the neck. The kid who had stuck his tongue out at me scampered away.

"Come on," said Alice, tugging at my sleeve. "We're not going to escape by jumping on a train."

"There's got to be another way," I said.

CHAPTER TWENTY-FOUR
APARTMENT 201

It was getting dark by the time we left the train station and I was bone-tired, thirsty, and utterly discouraged. The one highlight of the day was that toffee. "We're going to have to find someplace to sleep," I said.

"I have one possibility in mind," said Alice. "But it's a long walk."

Alice guided us uphill through city streets that had a dizzying mixture of houses that looked almost like palaces and other houses that were small and wooden. We passed stores and parks and more than one torn-down church. Having lived in a small village my whole life, seeing so many buildings so close together gave me a headache.

"Here we are," said Alice, stopping in front of a large, two-story brick house in the middle of a residential area. The house sat right at the edge of an intersection with not even the tiniest bit of space for a verandah or front step. I wondered whether in older times, this house would have had a garden or green space in front of it and maybe none of the smaller houses around it had even been built yet.

"What is this place?" I asked.

"This is where Papa and I lived when we first got to Kharkiv," said Alice.

"Here?" I asked, surprised. "It's huge."

"We didn't live here alone," she said. "It's a rooming house for foreigners."

"Do you know anyone here who might help us?" I asked.

"I wouldn't risk it," she said. "They could turn us in."

"Then why did we come here?"

"We're going to sleep here, and they won't even know it, but we have to time it right."

There was a broken-down house across the street, so we ended up sitting in the ruin of it, camouflaged behind some tall weeds and a rusted bed frame.

"Why don't we just sleep here?" I asked. I could feel my eyes getting heavy. I didn't know whether I'd be able to stay awake much longer.

"Garbage workers come at night, picking up the homeless and dead. You don't want to get picked up," she said.

We sat there waiting, trying to stay alert. Soon it was dark. The only illumination came from the lights inside the house across the street. A horse and trolley pulled up to the house and four men got out. They chatted among themselves as they opened the door and walked inside.

"Those are German specialists," Alice said. "They work at a factory right in Kharkiv. I don't know them very well because they don't speak English, but now they're home for the night. They'll be going to sleep soon."

A few minutes later, a girl with dark hair pulled back into a long ponytail and a stocky older woman came down the street and walked through the front door.

"That's Commandant Smirnova, the woman who runs the rooming house," said Alice. "And that's her grand-daughter, Olga, who was my best friend here. They must be coming home from a restaurant dinner."

"Do you think they might help us?" I asked.

"I wouldn't even ask," said Alice. "I'm sure Commandant Smirnova has already heard about Papa's arrest."

We sat there for another half hour, and the air became chilly. Then the light at the front door was turned off. Moments later, a light through a side window went off. Soon, the house was in darkness.

Alice led me around to the back of the house. We used the outhouse and quietly gulped water from the hand pump. I also splashed my face and hair with water to wash off the day's grime because we still wanted to keep ourselves presentable so the police didn't think we were farmers. "That feels so good," I whispered.

There was a small window with planks of wood nailed

across it. "We need to pry off the wood without waking anyone up," said Alice.

The wood was old and dry, so it didn't take much wriggling to get the nails to come loose. I went in first, then helped Alice.

It was too dark to get my bearings. "What is this room?" I whispered, feeling around with my fingertips. There was something about knee height that was cold and smooth.

"It's a bathroom," whispered Alice. "But the plumbing doesn't work, so the room was boarded off. No one comes in here."

It was a bathtub. I reached that way again and knocked away sticky wisps of what were probably cobwebs. "You get one end of the bathtub and I get the other," I said.

"That's what I was thinking," said Alice.

We both climbed in. Within minutes, I was sound asleep.

Sunlight pouring between the slats of wood across the window woke me up the next morning, and I did a double take when I saw a huge spider hanging about fifteen centimeters above my head. I guessed that he wasn't too happy about me ruining his web the night before. Alice was still asleep, and her eyes looked bruised with exhaustion. I stood up carefully, avoiding the spider and trying not to step on Alice. There was a mumble of voices from the other side of the wall so I put my ear against it to hear better.

"A meeting tonight and then we have the concert . . ."

"But I was supposed to go to Tatiana's tonight . . ."

"You can go tomorrow . . ."

Stomping feet. Slamming of a door . . .

"Eeek!" said Alice, jumping out of the tub. "There's a spider."

"Shhhh," I said, pointing to the wall. "There are people out there."

Alice covered her mouth with her hands and stepped over beside me. She put an ear to the wall but the conversation had finished. I hoped that was because they had left the room, not because they'd heard Alice shriek.

There was the squeak of a door opening, then banging shut. I looked between the slats of wood. The girl with the long dark ponytail was heading toward the outhouse.

As we waited in the bathroom for the people in the rooming house to get up and have their breakfast and leave, I tried to think of what we needed in the short term and what we needed in the long term.

Long term was simple to say but hard to do: get out of the country. Short term wasn't any easier. Each and every night we would need a safe place to sleep, and each and every day we would have to eat something. It didn't have to be a lot of food, but I knew from watching people starve around me that once the swelling started, the starvation had already set in. And once it started, it was hard to reverse. After that, even if you got food, your stomach couldn't handle it. Yesterday, we had each eaten one toffee and we had some water. What would we eat today? It wasn't the easiest thing to predict in the middle of such scarcity.

"The boarders are all gone now," said Alice. "It's safe for us to go out."

"Do you have any more of those toffees?" I asked.

"I have two," she said. "Let's save them for backup. Hopefully we'll be able to find something to eat today."

I pulled out the piece of paper with the teacher's address on it. "Do you know where this place is?"

She took the paper from me and looked at the address. "It's not far from here. Who is this person?"

"She's someone who helped my friend Roman, the son of our priest. Maybe she'll help us."

It turned out that Chaikov'ska Street was just a few big blocks over, but the area couldn't have been more different from the treed residential area of the rooming house. I stood still for a moment just to take it all in. There were no trees, no old houses. Instead, there were tall rows of new apartment buildings like the ones at the tractor plant.

We counted the buildings until we stood in front of the fourteenth. "Do you think we should just go inside and look for apartment 201?"

Alice shrugged. "What do we have to lose?"

The main floor was a wide dining area and kitchen, and the smell of baking bread made my stomach grumble.

The room was almost empty. Most people would be at work or school by this time in the morning, but there were still some people sitting here and there, with large chunks of bread and glasses of steaming tea.

Alice walked through the dining area as if she knew what she was doing, so I followed her. There were stairs at the back so we went up them. Apartment 201 was the very first door we encountered.

I rapped on it timidly, then waited.

No answer.

I knocked more firmly and we waited some more. Still no answer.

I turned to Alice. "There's no one home."

"Let's go down to the cafeteria and see if they might feed us," said Alice.

"Why would they?" I asked.

"We sometimes had guests at our dining hall at the tractor complex," said Alice. "Let me do the talking. What's this woman's name that we were supposed to be visiting?"

"Raisman," I said.

I followed Alice as she strode confidently over to the woman behind the kitchen window who was setting out plates of bread slathered with butter.

Alice stepped in behind a man who was in line. When he picked up a tray, she did the same, and so did I.

"Good day, Comrade Zaleska," the man said to the cook.

The woman nodded. He took one chunk of bread with butter and put it on his tray. He took a glass of tea. He walked away.

Alice approached the window. "Good day, Comrade Zaleska."

The woman looked up. "Who are you?" she asked.

"Alice White," she said, picking up one chunk of bread with butter and putting it on her tray.

"Who?" asked the woman.

"I'm Comrade Raisman's niece, visiting from Canada," said Alice. She grabbed a glass of tea and put it on her tray.

"Put that food down," shouted the woman.

"I am Alice White. I can show you my card."

"OUT," said the woman. She came around from the table and grabbed the tray from Alice. "Comrade Raisman was arrested for assisting kulaks."

I stepped in front of the table of bread, grabbed one chunk, and stuck it in my shoulder bag.

"You better get out of here now or I'll call the police."

Alice's face flamed bright red, but she strode to the door with her head held high. I was right behind her.

We were almost at the exit when the man who got served before us got up from his seat and blocked our way. He pointed to my bag.

"The bread that you stole," he said. "Give it back."

I tried to dash past him but he grabbed my arm. "Let go," I shouted.

He gripped my arm even harder.

Alice kicked him in the shin.

"Ow," he yelped. And he let go of me.

We raced out the door and stumbled out onto the street, weaving between the apartment buildings just in case Comrade Zaleska decided to call the police on us.

When we were away from the apartment complex, Alice slowed down. "I need to catch my breath," she said. "That was a bad idea."

"It was actually an excellent idea," I said. "We have bread." I patted my shoulder bag in triumph. "And she gave us valuable information on Roman's friend."

"Horrible information," said Alice.

"Yes," I said. "But it's better that we know. We can avoid this place now."

"How are we ever going to escape?" she said.

"We'll figure it out."

We ended up going back to the rooming house. As we walked there, I marveled at the fact that yesterday it was me in hopeless despair, but today it was Alice. Yesterday she had tried to bolster my mood, and today I was doing the same for her. We were a surprisingly good team.

We climbed back into the boarded-up bathroom because it was a place where we could eat without having starving people watch us. I broke our chunk of bread in half, and we savored each bite. More than once, I went out the window to have a long drink of water. Alice did the same.

We should have been figuring out what to do next, but we ended up talking instead. Alice told me about her life in Canada, and I told her what it was like in Felivka before the five-year plan.

And because we were in a private place, she took out the photographs to show me. Even though we were plunged in the midst of the hunger the photos depicted, seeing the suffering in black and white made it all the more real. "You're right," I said. "People won't ignore these photographs. They're proof of what Stalin's doing to his own people."

She kept one photograph back until the very end, and as she handed it to me, she said, "This one is special."

My breath caught in my throat when I saw what it was. My family. Everyone, except Uncle Illya. It had been taken on that day Alice and her papa had arrived in Felivka in the Packard. Mama, Tato, Slavko, Yulia, me, Auntie Pawlina, and Tanya, all lined up in front of our house and staring at the camera. So much had happened since this photograph was taken. "This is beautiful," I said.

"It's for you," said Alice.

I held it to my chest. "Thank you," I said.

CHAPTER TWENTY-FIVE
GOOD GARBAGE

We ended up spending a lot of nights at Alice's old rooming house although we tried never to stay in it two nights in a row. And even though food was tantalizingly close—the kitchen shared a wall with the bathroom—we didn't take any for risk of being caught and losing such a perfect sleeping place.

This boarded-off bathroom was safe and secluded as long as we stayed quiet when people were home, plus we had access to an outhouse and water pump. That allowed us to keep ourselves groomed and our clothing looking clean, which was essential to our goal of blending in with Young Pioneer kids instead of the street urchins. Every day we witnessed the police swooping down on kids from the country who were begging and stealing just like we were. I was determined to keep us safe.

We did a thorough cleanup of all the cobwebs so that neither of us had to wake up to the sight of a giant spider dangling down in our face.

None of the other places we stayed in were nearly as comfortable. One night we ended up in the crawl space under a doorstep, and once we took refuge inside a shattered church. Those nights were too terrifying for sleeping though. They were mostly about waiting until it was morning so we could go back to the rooming house bathroom after everyone there had gone off to work.

But we weren't making any headway in figuring out a way to escape the Soviet Union, and there was the constant challenge of finding something to eat every day. We were just two of many hungry people. That was the constant on the streets of Kharkiv—emaciated souls who had come to the city in hopes of finding food—but even the Komsomol members and the shock workers were having trouble now. They weren't starving, but they were feeling the pinch.

Usually we were able to scrounge or steal a morsel or a bite, but one night we came back to the rooming house bathroom and neither of us had eaten for more than twenty-four hours. Alice's legs were a little bit puffy, which meant that the beginning of starvation was dangerously close. I rolled up my pants. My legs were puffy too.

In the hopes of getting something to eat, we followed Olga and Commandant Smirnova to a restaurant for important people.

A man in an apron stood in the entrance.

"Commandant Smirnova, Olga, it's good to see you,"

he said. "Supper tonight costs one butter and one meat ration coupon each plus ten rubles each," he said.

The woman tore off the squares, counted the money, and handed it all to the aproned man and they were ushered into the restaurant.

"Come on," said Alice, tugging me by the sleeve.

We got up to the entrance and the waiter smiled in recognition. "I haven't seen you in a long time, Comrade Alice. Who's your friend?"

"This is my cousin, Nyl," said Alice. "We're doing some sightseeing around Kharkiv."

"Supper tonight costs one butter and one meat coupon each plus ten rubles each," said the waiter.

"Oh no," said Alice, searching through her bag and trying to look surprised. "I forgot my ration booklet and my wallet."

"You know I can't seat you without getting your stamps and cash," said the waiter.

"But you know who I am, and we're very hungry."

"I wish I could help you," said the waiter. "But you'll have to get your stamps and money and come back."

It looked like Alice was about to say something rude so I looped my hand through her elbow and tried to guide her away from the restaurant. The waiter stood watching, his hands on his hips.

We were about half a block away when the waiter finally went back inside.

"Even if we had stolen some stamps to use, there's no way we could waste ten rubles each on a restaurant meal," I said.

"The prices have gone up since I was here with Papa," said Alice. "Come on, let's get going."

She took a few steps down the street, looking utterly dejected.

"Wait," I said. "Let's go back."

"There's no point," said Alice. "He's not going to change his mind."

"No, but I bet they have really good garbage."

And they did. We rooted through the trash bin just outside their back door. We sucked on chicken bones that still had a bit of gristle on them and licked droplets of meat sauce off the side of the bin. I bit into an apple core, savoring its juicy sweetness and swallowing down the seeds and the stem. I found half a piece of white bread with butter on it. I tore it apart and gave Alice half.

It wasn't until we were nearly finished that I realized people from the restaurant could see us through the window. I elbowed Alice and pointed. There was Commandant Smirnova and Olga, watching us with disgust as they stuffed their own faces with chocolate cake.

The commandant flagged over the waiter, then pointed to us. We ran away before he came out the door.

"I hope they leave leftovers," said Alice. "That way, some other hungry people can eat tonight too."

CHAPTER TWENTY-SIX
TRUST

I had given up hope of ever finding Roman, but then one day at the market, I saw a flash of his distinctive eyeglasses in the crowd. I pushed my way through a dense bread line until I got to him. "Roman? Is that you?"

The boy turned around. "Nyl," he said. "It's good to see you." He was looking so clean and well fed that if it hadn't been for the glasses with the handle of a spoon across the bridge, I would have thought he was in the Komsomol. He looked at Alice, who stood beside me. "Who's your friend?"

"I'm Alice," she said. "From Canada."

Roman looked from her to me, frowning. "Canada? You're not the Young Pioneer girl, are you?"

"Long story, but yes," she said.

"She's trustworthy," I said.

"Let's get out of here," said Roman. "Follow me."

We went through narrow streets and between buildings, then climbed up a wooden ladder to the top of an abandoned building in the middle of what looked like a construction site.

"What is this place?" I asked.

"They're building a palace of culture, or maybe of sports," said Roman. "But the workers are on another project, so it's private here right now."

We talked about the fate of his teacher friend, Esther Raisman, and I told him about Mama's death and Slavko's decision to stay at the tractor plant. And then Alice showed him the photographs.

"We've got to get these out of the country," she said. "Convince people to stop buying Stalin's wheat."

"But we have no money for train fare," I said. "My auntie Pawlina and my cousin Tanya should be in Ternopil by now, and that's where we want to go."

"You need money," he said. And then he smiled. "Do you want me to show you some good stealing techniques?"

"Roman," I said in mock surprise. "What would your parents think, knowing that you're now living a life of crime?"

"Is it a crime to steal from the thief?" asked Roman. "We'll stake out the state store. The people who shop there are all Stalin's collaborators. I think my parents would rest easy with the thought of us making those murderers a little less comfortable."

We three blended in quite well—me with my shoulder bag and a devil's noose around my neck, Alice in a similar getup, and Roman looking tall and clean and relaxed.

"Just watch what I do and don't say a thing," said Roman.

We stepped into the line at the state store, with Roman in front and Alice and me just behind him. The person in front of him was a woman with a purse slung over her shoulder. He slipped his hand inside it so deftly that the woman didn't feel a thing when he lifted out her entire wallet. In a move that was like a magic trick, he stuck the wallet into my shoulder bag, then stepped out of the line. We followed him as he walked casually out of the market square and down a side street.

"Give me the wallet," he said.

I passed it to him.

He took out some of the cash and split it between us, then stuffed the ration stamps back inside it. "Don't ever try to use stolen ration stamps," he said. "You'll get caught for sure."

He didn't touch her identification papers either. He told us to follow him but to stay a couple meters back, and I watched in amazement as he passed right by the woman and dropped the wallet on the ground. Moments later, the person behind her picked it up and tapped her on the shoulder, asking if it was hers.

Roman kept on walking, and we followed him out of the square.

He had a similar method of stealing food right out of a person's shopping bag as they walked down the street. For the next few days, we used Roman's methods to steal from people who wouldn't miss it. He showed us some good places to sleep, and Alice and I slowly gained back some of our strength. But then one hot summer day it all fell apart.

CHAPTER TWENTY-SEVEN
STAGED

Trucks screeched into the market and police poured out. An officer hooked his arm around Alice's waist and lifted her off the ground.

I ran behind them. "Let her go!"

He threw her into the back of an open truck, and she screamed as she landed hard on the metal bed. He turned and grabbed me by the shoulders and threw me in practically on top of her. I swerved midair and missed her, but almost landed on top of the kid beside her.

We scrambled to the back of the truck bed as they tossed in more kids. Roman got thrown in next, his glasses flying off his face. I crawled over and grabbed them before they got crushed. Soon the truck bed was packed with screaming and terrified kids and it took off down the street.

I gave Roman his glasses. "Where are they taking us?" I asked.

"Jump out now while we still can," he said. "Before we get out of the city."

"But . . ."

Roman stood up, planting his feet wide to keep his balance. He reached down and grabbed Alice. "You're going first."

He picked her up and dropped her on the road. I watched her tuck her head in her arms and roll off the road, then run to hide. He grabbed me next and lowered me over the side. "Tuck and roll," he said.

The cobblestones grabbed my feet and I wrapped my arms around my head as I landed heavily onto my side. I rolled into the weeds at the side of the road.

Roman leapt out, lithe as a cat, then ran over to help me up. "Are you okay?" he asked.

"Just in shock," I said. "Where's Alice?"

She was trotting toward us, looking frazzled, with a scrape down the side of her face.

"Come on," said Roman. "We've got to get away from the road."

We hid behind a tumbledown house and watched the line of trucks pass by, each of them filled with terrified kids. A few jumped out like we had, disappearing among the buildings.

"It would have taken a long time to walk back if we hadn't jumped," said Roman. "They do these cleanups periodically, capturing all the homeless kids and dumping them outside the city. A lot of them are so weak they just die out there, but some make their way back."

"We need to stay off the street for now," I said. "The police could come back for us."

"I have a place we can go," said Roman. "Follow me."

The place he took us to was a rooming house quite similar to Commandant Smirnova's, except instead of sneaking in through a broken window, Roman used a key hidden in a flowerpot to open the front door.

"How is it that you know where the key is to this place?" I asked as we walked through the empty hallway and peered into the various rooms. Each one of them was lined with mattresses and bedrolls, and every space on the walls had clothing hanging from nails.

"I have a lot of friends who work long days, so their rental space is empty for sixteen hours at a stretch. I get to sleep in the hallway every now and again on the condition that I only do it during the day and I don't eat anyone's food. This is where my friend Timofey lives. I pay him back by bringing him food when I can. Come on upstairs, and we'll get cleaned up."

The upstairs was the same as the downstairs, with room upon room beehived with mattresses and bedrolls, and all the wall space covered with clothing on nails. Roman led us to a bathroom on the second floor that had running water and a flush toilet that worked. He gently washed off Alice's scratched cheek.

"We may as well try to get some sleep," said Roman. "We can't go outside because the police could be looking for us."

We each found a spot in the hallway to close our eyes and wait out the day. I quickly fell into a deep sleep and dreamt of a time when Roman was just my classmate and the priest's son, not someone who helped me steal and hide from the police. I woke up with a jolt at the sound of a key in the front door. We took off through the back before the front door opened.

When we went back to the market early the next morning, it had been transformed overnight. There were no bread lines and no urchins. The regular stores were locked up tight and dozens of colorful vendor stalls had been set up throughout the square. One stall sold sausages, another sold specialty Ukrainian breads, while another featured a pyramid of fresh shiny apples. In addition to all the food being sold, there were vendors displaying Ukrainian embroidery and scarves, carved wooden necklaces, and candlesticks and Russian matryoshka nesting dolls.

"We'd better hide," said Roman. "Something strange is going on here."

We found an unobtrusive spot on top of a building-in-progress that overlooked the market square. It gave us an excellent opportunity to see and hear what was going on below. Vehicles arrived and people assembled. There were men and women of all different ages, but one thing they had in common was they all looked like they'd just gotten out of bed. The men wore trunks and undershirts, and the women wore long sleeveless slips.

"When are they bringing the costumes?" asked one of the women. "I feel silly standing around in my slip."

"I don't know," said another. "But I can't speak Ukrainian. I'm just going to speak Russian and hope that these visitors don't know the difference."

Another truck pulled up, and an exhausted-looking woman jumped out of the passenger side. "The costumes are in the back," she said. "I need all the dancers to line up over there." She pointed to the right. "Musicians, stand with the dancers, and vendors, you need to be over there." She pointed to the left.

The driver hopped out and helped the wardrobe woman pass out the costumes. The dancers donned crisp new Ukrainian peasant skirts, embroidered blouses, and shiny red leather boots. They clipped coral beads around their necks and set wreaths of fresh flowers on top of their hair. The men's costumes were just as perfectly improbable, with matching colorful trousers, embroidered shirts, and tall red boots. Were these professional dancers? To me, they seemed like a postcard version of what village dancers really looked like. The musicians were each handed a balalaika, which no self-respecting Ukrainian musician would ever play because what tunes could you do with just three strings? The bandura, with its dozens of strings, is much better suited to complex folk melodies.

The actors who were supposed to dress as vendors were just as overdone. No one had everyday work clothing of plain, homespun shirt and bottoms. Instead, the women wore the kind of colorful embroidered blouses and woven wrap skirts that grandmothers might wear to church. Some of the men wore sheepskin vests even though it was summer, while others added another folksy touch, like smoking a long pipe or wearing a curly wool cap. They didn't look real.

Those playing vendors took their positions in the various stalls, while the people playing dancers and musicians wandered around and chatted. More people were brought in by truck and these ones were more plainly dressed, but they spoke Russian, not Ukrainian.

"How long do we have to stay here?" asked a woman.

"I've been paid for a full day, but maybe we can leave sooner," said another.

"I think we can leave once the foreigners are taken for refreshments," said a third.

The wardrobe woman clapped her hands and the chattering stopped. "Everyone, get into position," she said. "The visitors will be here in about five minutes." She pointed at the group under our window. "You," she said. "Stroll from stall to stall as if you were shopping."

"Can I eat some of that bread?" asked a voice.

"No. Most of the loaves are wooden. There are just enough real ones in case the foreigners decide to buy them." She clapped her hands again and shouted, "Action."

The actors stepped into their roles, wandering from stall to stall as if this were their real life.

A car pulled into the square about ten minutes into the performance. Two men in American suits and a woman in a frothy dress and delicate shoes got out and walked around in the market, chatting with the vendors and admiring the costumes of the dancers.

A musician began to play a Russian folk tune on the balalaika and the dancers assembled in the middle of the square for a dance.

The woman tourist said something in English and clapped her hands in glee. Alice whispered to Roman and me, "She says she's so excited to witness how native Ukrainians spend their days and is particularly pleased that they happened to be here when the natives broke out in spontaneous dance."

We stayed in our second-floor window and watched the fake "authentic" dancing. One of the men got out a camera and took photographs. After it was over, the tourists bought some souvenirs, and an actor gifted them with one of the breads that wasn't wooden. Then they were escorted to a nearby hotel.

After they left, I slumped down on the wood floor. "You know what this means, don't you?" I asked Alice.

"What?"

"They'll go back to America with their 'authentic' pictures of what it's like here. There's no starvation or repression. I bet there are performances like that happening all over the countryside."

"All the more reason for me to get Papa's photos out," said Alice.

Within days of the tourists leaving, the market was back to its usual self: the snaking line in front of the three official stores, the cobblestones cluttered with ragged and emaciated souls from the country, and those with access to food pretending the mounds they stepped over weren't dying humans.

Alice and I blended right in with Roman's cadre of pickpockets, feeding ourselves but also helping others like us find comfort, food, and refuge in the hidden places all over the city that the Stalinists overlooked. We were slowly accumulating cash one kopek at a time with the hope of finally getting out, but it was hard enough to steal sufficient food, let alone save spare money for a trip. Mostly, the money we saved went toward buying food for someone who would die without it. Even so, every night the corpse collectors came and loaded up our dead friends like so much trash. That was something I would never get used to.

Alice and I spent a lot of time near the American hotel because we'd watch for the restaurant to put out its delicious trash. One day in August we saw an unusual sight: three American women in an automobile, and one of the women was driving. It was rare to see a car at all, and I had never seen a woman driver. She parked the car in front of the American hotel. A valet took the keys from her, and the three women went inside.

We snuck into the lobby and watched from the shadows as each of the women were given separate room keys. They chatted as they walked down the hallway.

"The driver is Canadian," whispered Alice.

"How do you know?" I asked.

"Her accent is like mine," said Alice. "I wouldn't be surprised if she's from Toronto, just like me."

"Maybe she would drive us out of the Soviet Union."

CHAPTER TWENTY-EIGHT
RHEA

We shadowed the three women the whole next day to get a sense of what they were up to. The driver did things on her own and the two others stuck together, so we split up and Alice followed the driver and I followed the other two.

My day was boring. The two women spoke only English, so I had no idea what they were saying, but also they were only interested in shopping and eating. I stood behind walls and posts and watched as they tried on clothing in fancy shops, bought exotic food at the Torgsin, and haggled with starving farmers for an antique ring or a necklace.

"My day was great," said Alice when we met up later. "I was able to eavesdrop on a number of conversations she's had with locals. Her name is Rhea and she's a journalist. Plus, I was right, she's from Toronto."

"Did the Stalinists put on some plays for her?" I asked.

"Not this time," said Alice. "She's on this trip without anyone from the government. She went inside factories and interviewed farmers herself. She doesn't speak Ukrainian, but she's fluent in Russian. I don't think anyone's fooling her."

"That's impressive," I said. "Are you going to ask her if she'll get us out of the country?"

"Yes," she said. "I heard her say that she's leaving tomorrow, so we'll have to ask her tonight. She's out for dinner right now, so we should wait for her to come back."

We snuck into the hotel and waited in the shadows close to Rhea's hotel room. When Rhea came back from supper, she passed so close to us when she walked down the hallway that I could have touched her sleeve if I had put out my hand. Once she was in her room, we counted to a hundred and then Alice went up to Rhea's door and knocked.

I crept closer. Rhea opened the door. She looked at Alice and said in Russian, "I'm sorry but I have no food for you." Alice said something to her in English. I don't know what it was exactly, but it included the words *Canadian* and *Toronto*.

Rhea gasped. She opened the door wide and gestured for Alice to step in. I got out of the shadows. "May I come in too?" I asked in Russian so she'd understand me. "My name is Nyl and I'm Alice's friend, but I don't speak English."

Rhea looked surprised, but she said in Russian, "That's fine. Come in."

The room had a table with chairs by the window so we sat there, and I listened as Alice spoke in Russian, telling Rhea the story of how she and her father decided to come to the Soviet Union to help Stalin but then they gradually realized how his plans were killing people.

"I was idealistic just like you when I first came here," said Rhea. "It's been a shock to find out the truth."

"My father was arrested as a traitor for taking these photographs," said Alice, pulling them from her bag and fanning them out on the table.

Rhea picked up one and then another and examined them carefully. "These photographs clearly show what's happening here."

"Can we leave with you in your car?" asked Alice. "We need to get out of the country so we can tell the world what Stalin is doing."

"I can't do that," said Rhea. "It took a lot of planning and coordination for me to do this huge cross-country journey through the famine lands, and I've just begun. It's dangerous but important that I personally take photographs and write in the newspapers about what I see with my own eyes."

Alice slumped down on the chair. "I guess my father shouldn't have risked his life taking these pictures, then, if you say they're not necessary."

"You are also a witness," said Rhea. "The Soviets are destroying photographs when they find them. The more that get out, the better. It's just that I can't stop my trip to drive you out of the country."

"I appreciate what you're doing," said Alice. "It is very important. But you were our last hope."

"We've been trying to save money for train fare to Ternopil," I said. "But we barely have enough day to day to survive."

"Ternopil?" asked Rhea. "Why would you think it's a good idea to go there?"

"It's outside the Soviet Union," I said. "And it's the only place I have family."

"Let me show you something," said Rhea, getting up and rooting through some papers. She came back holding a hand-drawn map and spread it out on the table. "This is where we are," she said, putting a finger on Kharkiv.

"I know," said Alice. She set her finger onto Ternopil. "And this is where we need to go. There's a British embassy in Poland. I can get back to Canada, report Papa's arrest. And I know that it's nearly eight hundred kilometers, which is why we need a lot of money to get there."

"Do you know where the famine is?" asked Rhea.

"In all the places in the Soviet Union with farms."

"No," said Rhea. "It's not in the Russian parts, only in the parts where Ukrainians live. If you want to get out of the famine, you only need to go sixty-five kilometers north, to the border between Ukraine and Russia. As soon as you cross that border into Russia, the famine ends."

"How is that possible?" I asked. "Aren't the farms in Russia also being collectivized?"

"I've seen what's been happening with my own eyes," said Rhea. "Stalin is collectivizing farms all over, but he's targeting Ukrainians for extinction. They're being starved to death, executed, exiled to slave labor camps in the north."

"But why would he do that?" asked Alice.

"He wants Ukrainian land but not Ukrainian culture and traditions. He wants the Soviet Union to be Russian."

Her words stunned me.

"But we're Ukrainian," I said. "Won't we be stopped crossing the border into Russia?"

Rhea sat back and looked at us both, and her brow wrinkled in thought. "Alice," she said. "I assume you're a Young Pioneer."

"I am," said Alice. "I have my necktie and pin. I also have my Canadian birth certificate and Soviet identification papers. I don't have my passport, because it was confiscated when we arrived."

"All the more reason not to go to Ternopil," said Rhea. "The Soviets would shoot you at the border."

"I have a Young Pioneer necktie and pin too," I said.

"But you're from a Ukrainian village, aren't you?" asked Rhea. "So you don't have Soviet identification papers. They don't give those to Ukrainian villagers."

I pulled my papers from my pocket and put them on the table. "Alice's father made me these counterfeit ones."

Rhea opened the booklet and examined it carefully. Her eyebrows rose. "He did a good job," she said. "You can travel through the Soviet Union with these. You've got to remember to speak Russian, though, not Ukrainian."

"Getting into Russia means that we'll escape the hunger," said Alice. "But I will be no further ahead in getting my photographs seen by the right people."

"You'll need to get yourself to Moscow," said Rhea. "To the British embassy there."

I looked at the map. "Moscow is just as far away as Ternopil," I said.

"But you'll be out of the famine area in sixty-five kilometers," said Rhea. "That's key."

Rhea left the next day with the two other women as she had planned, but she paid for an extra night on the hotel room so we could stay to rest and recuperate before our big trip.

"There's hot water for that bathtub," she said. "Clean yourselves up."

She also got us food: dried fruit and cheese and bread that would travel well, but also delectably soft bread and fatty kobasa that we could eat once she had gone.

"I'm on my way to Tractorzloy," she said. "If there's any news about your father, I'll write about it in the papers."

"Thank you for all your help," said Alice.

"Dress in your Young Pioneer uniforms and speak Russian. Good luck and Godspeed," she said.

After Rhea left, we snuck Roman into the hotel room and the three of us shared the soft bread and kobasa and we stayed up all night planning. I drew a map like Rhea's and begged Roman to cross the border with us, but he refused.

"If I leave, who will help the street kids to survive?" he asked.

That night, Roman and I slept on one of the beds and Alice got the other. After all this time of being on the run, it felt strange to have a soft pillow under my head and a cover on top of me. It also felt luxurious to be so clean. I closed my eyes and the image of my map was crisp in my mind. The Russian border was tantalizingly close. Just by crossing it, I'd have food again. When I thought we were going to Ternopil, I had looked forward to reuniting with Auntie Pawlina and Tanya. I had also reconciled myself to never seeing my brother or sister again, but with food and freedom just sixty-five kilometers away, that changed everything. I could visit Slavko, maybe even carry food to him. And it left the door open for Yulia as well. Maybe we'd all be together again in the future.

But first, I needed to help Alice get over the border and in contact with someone at the British embassy. She had to get those photographs out and she had to try to free her father.

CHAPTER TWENTY-NINE
A GIRL WITH NO NAME

We had a tearful goodbye with Roman the next morning, then packed our bags with food, an empty tin can to use as a drinking cup, our papers, the little money we'd managed to save, and the photographs. Alice put her hair in a tidy braid and looped her Red Pioneer tie around the collar of her newly washed blouse. I slicked my clean hair back with water and put my own red devil's noose onto my own clean collar. We walked past the train station and went north, first following the tracks, and then on a dirt road that paralleled the tracks. My inclination had been to travel with the road in sight but not on it, because it felt like what we were doing had to be hidden. But Alice pointed out that doing so would make us look like we had something to hide. Better to walk on the road, our day bags over our shoulders, like loyal Communists with a place to go.

Once we got into the country, the air smelled different. It took me a while to realize that it wasn't just because there were trees and streams and wide-open spaces, but because there was no all-pervasive stench of rotting corpses.

As we walked, I thought about the journeys I had made with Slavko. Back then, it was about keeping our family together, and safe. Now my parents were dead and this trip took me farther away from my siblings. The kolkhoz at Felivka was Yulia's home but definitely not mine, and our shattered house had likely been torn down by now. Slavko considered Tractorzloy his home, while to me it was a place of punishment, not refuge. I had pinned my hopes on a new home with Auntie Pawlina in Ternopil, but that dream had fallen through too.

Would I ever find home again?

I took a deep breath, then slowly let it out. I would concentrate on what I could do instead of worrying about what I couldn't.

I glanced over at Alice, who was as silent as me and had a serious look on her face. She still had a home and a grandmother in Canada and it was possible she might be able to save her father. And I would help her in any way I could. "What are you thinking about?" I asked.

"About how beautiful this all was," she said, raising her arms to include the sky, the fields, the meadows. "There is so much potential for happiness, for goodness here."

"You're right about that," I said.

We walked in silent contemplation for a couple of

kilometers, then encountered a village. The clay cottages with their straw-thatch roofs seemed achingly familiar, and in normal times I would have expected to see some chickens clucking around and maybe a cow in the pasture, but these were not normal times. In the heat of August, the village was quiet like winter. No people. No birds. No insects.

We followed the dirt road deeper into the village and I wrinkled my nose at the stench. Alice put a hand over her mouth. She could smell it too. It was fainter than in Kharkiv, but unmistakable. At a time of year when everything should be bursting with life, this village was filled with death.

We kept on walking, our heads bowed in sadness, past what had been the village square and past where a church had been but now was just rubble. Reclining against the doorstep of the last house was a young girl, maybe six years old. At first I thought she was dead, but then she slowly opened her eyes. Her lips moved, but no words came out.

We went up to her and knelt beside her.

"Bread?" she whispered.

I opened my shoulder bag. I had a small piece of the soft bread left from the night before. I placed it in her hand. The girl tried to bring it to her lips but she was too weak. I broke off a bit and put it between her teeth, but her mouth was too dry. Alice took the tin can from her bag and went to the back of the house. She reappeared moments later, the tin can filled with water. She held it to the girl's lips.

The girl took a sip. Once she'd swallowed a bit of water, I placed the bread back on her tongue. She closed her mouth and slowly chewed. A smile transformed her face.

"That is the most wonderful meal I have ever tasted," said the girl. "I can die happy now." We stayed sitting with the girl and offered her more bread, but she said that she was full. "Can you sing to me?" she asked.

I have a terrible singing voice but started a kolysanka that Mama sang to me as a baby about rocking in a cradle. It was one that Uncle Illya and Auntie Pawlina had recorded in their manuscript. Alice knew it too, and she joined in. The little girl looked so content that we sang it over and over. I thought the girl had fallen asleep but Alice put her fingers on the girl's neck. "She is no longer with us," she said.

We didn't want to leave her sitting in the doorway. In the end, I carried her gently in my arms to the church cemetery and laid her body down on one of the graves. Alice and I wrapped our arms around each other and wept. We had been immersed in death for so long that I thought we had become hardened to it, but seeing this little girl die before our eyes was a breaking point.

"We don't even know her name," I said.

"She wasn't alone when she died," said Alice. She gathered up a handful of dirt and sprinkled it over the girl. Together we sang "Vichnaya Pamyat."

And then we walked out of the village and down the road.

There were more than a dozen villages between the outskirts of Kharkiv and the border between Ukraine and Russia, and all of those villages were terrible in their similarities: like winterkill in the heat of August. The stench of death, the emptiness, and a harvest without food.

At one of the villages, a grizzled old man took us into his house. He told us that during the harvest the locals were too weakened with starvation to go out in the fields and work, so the army brought in Russian farmers to do the harvest. "The army fed the Russian farmers so little that they all got sick," he said. "But at least they got something."

"What about your garden?" asked Alice. "Don't you at least have tomatoes, potatoes?"

"They've taken everything," said the man. "Even if they find you picking up dropped ears of wheat, they'll shoot you."

"How is it that you're still alive?" I asked.

"Take a look," he said, taking the lid off a foul-smelling cooking pot. Grass, weeds, a leather boot, one dead rat, all boiling together in water. "That's what I've got left. Come winter I'll die."

Our food would have lasted the entire three days and sixty-five kilometers had we not shared, but how could we not? We did have our tin cup and we drank water whenever we could. When we were about ten kilometers from the border, Alice said, "I need to rest."

"We should just keep walking," I said. "If we stop when we're so weak, we won't get back up."

But it was too late. Alice's knees buckled beneath her and she crumpled onto the road. "I just need to rest my eyes," she said. "I'm so tired."

"Okay," I said. "But just for a few minutes."

I helped her to the side of the road, then rolled my coat into a pillow and placed it under her head. I sat down beside her and wrapped my arms around my knees. My intention was to stay awake and keep watch, but I fell asleep.

When I woke up, I was in a donkey cart that was jolting and swaying along a rutted road. An old man walked alongside the donkey, his hand looped around the strap to a leather harness. Alice lay beside me, loose like a discarded rag doll. I put my hand on her wrist and felt her pulse beat strongly. I said a silent prayer of thanks. Another kid lay still and cold in death, and I whispered a prayer for him as well. I crawled back over to Alice and tried to shake her awake. I desperately wanted to get out of this death wagon, but I couldn't leave Alice.

Just then, the cart stopped. I slumped down and closed my eyes, pretending to be dead. I could hear the man's boots swishing through the field, then him picking something up with a grunt. A few minutes later, a body crashed down on me.

The donkey started back on its slow walk.

I opened my eyes to the sight of brown eyes clouded with death staring back at me. The body was so light that it was like moving a bundle of firewood when I squirmed out from beneath him. I gently rolled him over beside the other corpse, then went to check on Alice. She was still breathing, but also still deep in sleep.

The wagon took a sharp turn, then climbed a hill. I lay down between Alice and the corpses when it stopped.

The man came around to the back of the wagon and grabbed one of the dead kids. I heard a whoosh and a thump. A few moments later, he grabbed me. I kept my eyes closed and tried to keep my body slack. He tossed me down a hill. My back hit the ground first. I tucked in my arms and kept rolling, then stopped abruptly when I smacked up against something hard.

Maybe the man would shoot me if he knew I was alive, so I lay there playing dead as the rot of death filled my nostrils. Another body rolled on top of me, and then Alice smashed down.

"What, what . . ." said Alice, her eyes fluttering open. Thank goodness she was finally awake.

"Shhh," I whispered. "Pretend you're dead."

Miraculously, she didn't scream or gasp, but just went silent. We waited there in the vast death pit, amid the bodies for fifteen minutes or more.

I stared up at the hot blue August sky and saw ravens

circling above. It reminded me of the ravens that hovered over the mass grave where Tato's body was discarded. My heart ached at the thought of so many dead people and fat crows.

"Can we get up yet?" asked Alice.

"He's probably gone by now," I said, standing up myself, then helping Alice to her feet. We slowly took in the horror around us. A vista of sun-bleached skulls and bones as far as the eye could see. Thrown like so much rubbish on top were fresher bodies. How many mass graves were there throughout the countryside?

"Let's get out of here," said Alice.

I knew that horrible climb through the pit of death would stay etched in my nightmares forever, but even amid all that destruction was a glimmer of hope. A small hand stretched out toward us, cold and still in death, but with fingers gripped around a piece of rough black bread.

"Would it be sacrilege to take that?" I asked.

"It would be sacrilege not to," said Alice.

We stood there among the dead and I broke off two small pieces of bread. Just enough to stave off the swelling. I said a prayer of thanks.

When we got out of the pit, I didn't know which way to go.

"North is this way," said Alice, using the sunset to orient us.

We walked as far away from the pit as we could get while it was still light enough to do so. We found a stream to slake our thirst, and then crumpled into the field and slept.

At dawn, we walked again. And walked and walked. Another stream and more water. Another bite of bread.

It was hours later when we heard the gunshots.

CHAPTER THIRTY
THE BORDER

Alice pulled me behind a tree and put a finger to her lips. We were near a border crossing into Russia. A couple of Soviet soldiers stopped each person and questioned them before they let them go through. As we watched, a man on a horse approached the border. He handed a paper from his pocket to the soldier. The soldier looked at the paper, then handed it back. They waved him through.

"We have our papers," said Alice. "Let's walk through."

We stepped onto the road and walked toward the border crossing.

"Stop there," said the younger of the soldiers, who had unruly sandy hair sticking out from under his cap. "I need to see your papers."

He looked at mine, then handed it back. "Thank you, Comrade," I said.

He paused at Alice's papers. "You're Canadian?"

"Yes," she said, in Russian.

"How do you like it here?" he asked.

"Beautiful country," she said, a smile pasted onto her face.

The soldier grinned and nodded. "We have much to be proud of," he said. "Go on in."

"Thank you," said Alice. As she put away her papers, she looked back up at the soldier and asked, "I thought we heard gunshots a few minutes ago. Is there anything we should be worried about?"

"No," he said. "It was just some kulaks trying to get across. Other than that, this crossing is pretty boring."

"I'm relieved," said Alice.

We walked past the border mark and into Russia.

Once we were out of the soldiers' sights, I sat down on a rock at the side of the road. Alice sat down beside me and clutched one of my hands in both of hers.

"They shot people who were just looking for food," I said.

Alice squeezed my hand but didn't reply. From the sound of her breathing, I knew that she was weeping.

A half day later, our road took us through a small village that was bordered by a creek with willows and apple trees along its banks. It looked so much like our own river and orchards that my heart was overcome with a longing for home. We followed the road and the creek to the end of the village and then through a quiet wooded area.

"Let's cool our feet off," I said to Alice, leading her down a path to the creek.

The water was icy but felt soothing on our swollen, blistered feet, and I reveled in the sound of the water, the croaking of frogs and the songs of the birds. It seemed like life was bursting all around us.

We put our shoes back on and continued through the woods. We encountered a thatch-roof cottage. A man sat on a wood stump peeling the skin off an apple with a knife so sharp that it glinted in the dappled sunlight.

I grabbed Alice's elbow and pulled her behind a tree. "Hide," I whispered.

"I'm not going to hurt you," he called out.

We stepped out from behind the tree.

The man sliced his apple in half, put the knife in his back pocket, then walked over to us. He handed us each half an apple.

Alice let out a strangled thank-you as she reached for her piece of apple.

"Thank you," I said, holding my apple half up to my face and breathing in its rich scent. I took a small bite and closed my eyes, reveling in its sweetness. I was overwhelmed with gratitude, with sadness. After all the death and casual cruelty we had lived through on our journey north to Russia, this small act of kindness pierced through my defenses.

"Come and sit for a bit," he said, leading us back toward his house and setting up two more wood stumps.

"This is so nice of you," said Alice, sitting on one of the stumps and taking small nibbles of her apple half. I sat down beside her.

"You can stay in my barn for one night," said the man. "I'll give you more to eat today and breakfast tomorrow, but I get kulaks coming across all the time, and I can't afford to have anyone stay for long."

"We're very grateful," I said.

"I'd kick Stalin in the behind if I could," said the man, spitting on the ground. "Starving the Ukrainians, it's crazy."

The man gave us just a couple of spoonfuls of plain kasha for supper. "Your stomach can't handle any more, I've learned that from experience," he said.

The next morning, after more kasha, we were on our way with a warning to avoid the Orlov farm but to definitely stop by the Ivanovs'.

For days we wandered along the smaller dirt roads, roughly going north, closer to Moscow. We begged hospitality from kind strangers, staying with each Russian family for a night, sometimes two.

All during the hunger, the only Russians I had met had been the ones sent in from Moscow to punish us and steal from us. These country Russians, with their hospitality and practical compassion, were a refreshing change. It was good to know that Stalin's speeches and cartoon posters of kulaks hadn't infected everyone.

"There's an old woman named Anna who lives on her own and could use the company and some help," said a widow named Luda, who had let us stay for two days in exchange for chopping firewood and helping with her canning. "Go that way for a kilometer." She thrust a small burlap sack into my hands. "Give her this. Tell her it's from Luda."

"Thank you for everything," I said, shaking Luda's hand. Alice gave her a big hug.

Anna's thatch-roof cottage didn't take long to get to, and I could see even from a distance why Luda thought Anna would welcome our company. Her barn was in terrible shape, half of it collapsed from the wind, and it looked like her vegetable garden had gotten the better of her, with too much produce for just one old woman to harvest, chop, and preserve.

She was sitting on her front step mending a shirt when we arrived, but she looked up from her work and noticed us.

I held up the burlap sack. "Luda asked us to bring these to you," I said.

Anna smiled. She took the bag from me and wrapped a gentle arm around each of us and led us inside her house.

"You must be good workers for Luda to trust you with her prized dried mushroom mix. I've got lots of work here for you in exchange for food and a place to sleep if you'd like to stay."

Her place looked so much like home, with the tall clay wood-burning pich and the lime-washed sleeping platforms. She settled us onto kitchen chairs and made us hot mint tea with a little bit of honey and gave us each a thick piece of rye bread.

"You're probably still not used to eating a lot, so take it slowly."

CHAPTER THIRTY-ONE
RAVENS AND FLOWERS

It seemed that during every moment of the last three years all I could think about was staying alive and protecting my family. On our journey out of the famine lands I concentrated on just one thing, and that was getting Alice over the border alive. We had crossed the border. We were alive. We had food and a safe place to live. Anna was almost like a mother to us with her loving care and generosity. Through all the hunger and sadness, I kept on going, willing myself not to think or feel, but now that we were safe, I fell apart.

While I repaired Anna's barn and chopped firewood for the winter, I mourned the deaths of Tato, Mama, Uncle Illya, and the priest's family. I felt guilty about abandoning Slavko. I even felt guilty about Yulia. Maybe if I had spent more time with her, she wouldn't have felt the need to become such a little Stalinist.

I was overcome with sadness and had a deep need to sleep and mourn. A similar transformation was happening with Alice. She brought in all the vegetables from the garden and wept as she helped Anna can and stew and dry them for the winter. Alice told me that she felt tremendous guilt about all the inventories she had taken and all the people labeled kulaks because of her lists. She worried about her father's fate and wondered how her grandmother was faring all alone in Toronto. Even though I was going through the same kind of emotions myself, it shocked me to see Alice fall apart. Anna took it in stride. "I had a Ukrainian stay with me last winter," she said. "After all that he lived through, it wasn't until he was safe that the emotions settled in. He got through it, and so will you."

She praised us for the work we did and fed us small meals of nourishing food and made sure we got lots of sleep.

In January 1933, Anna came back from the market with the news that Stalin had sealed the borders around Ukraine and he made it illegal for Ukrainian farmers to leave their village. Without food and with no way of getting any, was it now their duty to die in place?

I was grateful that Alice and I had gotten out when we did, but my heart was sick at the thought of Yulia still in Felivka. It didn't matter if you had joined a kolkhoz or resisted—all rural Ukrainians were enemies now, and all were slated for starvation. And what of Slavko? The conditions at the tractor plant had been horrible when I left and they would only get worse, but it was better to be at the tractor plant than in the village. Stalin wanted tractors. I hoped and prayed that Slavko would live.

We were enveloped in snow, and the weeks slipped by. Entire days were slept away. During that hazy time, when I was awake, the pictures on Anna's walls seemed larger than life. There was of course the obligatory one of Stalin and another of Lenin, but she also had a faded photo of a young woman and man sitting formally side by side and staring solemnly out at the camera.

Anna saw me staring at it one day so she took it down and brought it to my bedside. "That's me," she said. "Our engagement picture."

"Your husband?" I asked, pointing to the man.

"Yevgeny was shot and killed during the Russian Revolution," she said. "Our son, Leo, was just a baby. I had him and Yevgeny's parents to look after all on my own."

"Where's Leo now?" I asked.

"Moscow," she said. "He works at a factory. That's where he met Marusia, his wife."

"Do they visit often?" I asked.

"A few times a year," she said.

When Alice was stronger, she took out her father's photographs and showed them to Anna.

"This is so bad," said Anna. "I don't understand why Stalin is doing this. Ukrainians are our brothers and sisters. Marusia, my own daughter-in-law, is part Ukrainian."

"My father was arrested for taking these pictures," said Alice. "I need to get to Moscow. To the British embassy there. They need to see these. They need to help Papa."

"It's not so hard to take the train from here to Moscow," said Anna. Now that we were out of the famine zone, the train fares weren't inflated. Our pickpocket money from the streets of Kharkiv was enough for a single one-way ticket.

"That's perfect," I said. "You only need to go one way, and you should leave as soon as you feel healthy enough."

"But what about you?" asked Alice. "Aren't you coming with me?"

"That would only complicate things," I said. "You'll be leaving for Canada." I turned to Anna. "With your permission I'd like to stay with you for a bit longer. I want to contact Slavko and let him know where I am. Maybe he'll cross the border too. That means staying in the same place for a while."

"You can stay with me for as long as you want," said Anna. "I appreciate your company and your help."

As we saw Alice off at the train depot, I felt like my heart had been torn in two. I had resented Alice for a long time, but in the end she had become like a sister. "Please write," I said, hugging her tight. "I want to know that you're safe. I want to know if your father is still alive."

"I'll write to you when I get back to Canada," she said. "But remember, there are censors. If I mention ravens in my letter, that means that Papa is either dead or in a slave labor camp."

"What about the photographs?" I asked. "How will you tell me if you get someone important to look at them?"

"Flowers," she said.

Just before stepping onto the train, she thrust an envelope into my hand. I shoved it into my pocket, then waved once she found a seat on the train and sat down.

When Anna and I got back home, I opened the envelope. It was a photograph of Alice standing in front of the rooming house in Kharkiv where we'd taken refuge in the broken bathroom. Her father must have taken it before they began living at the tractor plant. She had looked so hopeful back then—so young too. I opened up my leather bag and withdrew the photograph she'd given me before, of my family in Felivka from when Mama and Tato were still alive. I set the photographs on the table so Anna could see them both.

"This is your mama?" she asked, putting her index finger over the shadow on Mama's eyes as if she could brush away the worry.

"It is," I said. "And this is Tato."

"And the sister who betrayed you, and Slavko, who loves tractors," she said, tapping the faces with her finger.

"Yes," I told her. "This is Auntie Pawlina, who I hope is in Ternopil now, and my cousin Tanya."

"Such a sweet child," said Anna. "Reminds me of Leo when he was little." She picked up the photograph of Alice and smiled. "This is a brave girl."

"She is," I said. "I hope she gets home safely."

"You've done a good job," said Anna.

"What do you mean?" I asked. "My parents are dead; my siblings are scattered."

"But you saved your aunt and cousin. You saved Alice too. Yulia and Slavko made their own choices. You concentrated on what you could do instead of being distracted by what you couldn't."

Her words were like a salve to my heart. "Thank you," I said.

I mailed a letter to Slavko, telling him where I was and letting him know that I missed him. In the end I also wrote a letter to Yulia. I didn't know what to say because I was still angry with her, but I wished her well and hoped she was healthy. I also sent a letter to Auntie Pawlina in Ternopil, letting her know that I was out of the famine zone and that Slavko was at the tractor plant.

As the last bits of snow were melting in the woods, a

letter arrived from Auntie Pawlina. Her words were carefully chosen to evade being censored by the government but she still managed to tell me everything I needed to know:

Dear Nyl,

> *Knowing that both of my nephews are alive has made my heart sing.*
> *Please know that you always have a home with me. Your cousin Tanya sends a kiss.*
> *With love,*

> *Auntie*

Winter ended and spring arrived, but no letter came from Canada. Then, in July, I finally heard from Alice. When I opened the envelope, a photograph fell out.

It was a picture of Alice looking strong and healthy. She stood beside a friendly-looking woman whom I recognized as her grandmother. In the background was a brick house with flowers in the garden.

Flowers.

Someone important was interested in the famine photographs.

I collapsed into a chair. Relief washed over me.

Her letter was short:

Dear Nyl,

Thank you for being my friend. Hope that we'll meet again in the future.
Always,

Alice

No mention of ravens. I flipped the paper over just to make sure, but the back of it was blank. I looked at the photograph again. No ravens. That meant Comrade White wasn't in a prison camp and hadn't been executed.

A wave of relief passed over me.

Anna came in just then and set a basket of berries on the table. "You look happy," she said.

"Not quite happy," I said. "But I am hopeful." I wrapped my arms around this woman who had been a stranger but who had taken me in and nurtured me back to health through a long, cold winter. "Thank you for your friendship."

Stalin hadn't killed me—he just made me stronger. I would go home to my family when the timing was right, but no matter when that happened, I would always be grateful for my friends.

AUTHOR'S NOTE

A brief history of the Holodomor

The word *Holodomor* literally translates to "murder by hunger."

Millions died in Soviet Ukraine between the fall of 1932 and the spring of 1933 when Stalin, the dictator of the Soviet Union, ordered all food to be removed from Ukrainian rural homes; he then had the borders sealed and ordered anyone who tried to escape to be shot.

According to slick Soviet propaganda, Ukrainian farmers were depicted as selfish and fat, with greasy skin and tanned complexions. They were labeled "kulaks," a demeaning and racist term.

Stalin demanded "the liquidation of the kulaks as a class."

Starting in 1929, a million and a half Ukrainian farmers were either deported to slave labor camps in Siberia or executed on the spot. At the same time, Stalin imprisoned and killed Ukraine's intellectual leaders, including artists, writers, teachers, and academics. Stalin also imprisoned and killed Ukrainian Orthodox clergy and tore down church buildings.

From 1930 to 1932, under the guise of combining privately owned farms into giant government-owned collectives, rural homes were scoured top to bottom and every kernel of grain was confiscated by the military. After that, Communist brigades went from home to home and took any food that remained. Anyone who resisted was labeled a kulak and either shot or deported. Even many of those who joined the collective farms eventually starved as the Holodomor progressed.

In January 1933, the borders around Ukraine were sealed and a passport system was set up, but Ukrainian farmers were not allowed passports and were not allowed to leave their villages. Those caught fleeing were taken back to their villages to die.

Some of the confiscated wheat rotted in government warehouses. Some was made into alcohol. Much was sold abroad.

After the Holodomor, settlers from Russia and Belarus were brought in to repopulate the starved-out Ukrainian villages.

Total death estimates are in the millions, including millions of children. It's impossible to know the exact number because those who documented it were executed.

The Soviets suppressed the news of the Holodomor by bribing foreign journalists. The most notorious liar was Walter Duranty of the *New York Times*, who spoke privately about the millions who had been starved to death but publicly wrote that there was no famine. Duranty received the Pulitzer Prize for his false articles. That award has never been revoked.

Rhea Clyman was one of the few courageous journalists who reported what she saw, even though she risked her life and her career by doing so. Malcolm Muggeridge and Gareth Jones are two other brave and principled journalists who told the truth despite the risk.

Inspiration for Rhea, Alice, and Nyl

Just like the character Rhea in the novel, Rhea Clyman herself traveled by car through the famine areas of Soviet Ukraine, taking photographs, interviewing, and documenting.

Alice is inspired by a girl named Alice whom Rhea met in her hotel in Kharkiv in August 1932. Like my character, the real Alice was from Toronto and her father came to Kharkiv to work at the tractor plant.

Nyl is named after my own son, Neil. His experiences and that of his family and fellow villagers are based on my face-to-face interviews with survivors, as well as first-person survivor accounts that I've read and listened to.

I also used first-person accounts of workers, foreign specialists, Komsomol members, Young Pioneer members, and the Communist elite to re-create day-to-day life in the village, in Kharkiv, and at the tractor plant.

The final stretch of Nyl's sixty-five kilometer trek north with Alice is inspired by Welsh journalist Gareth Jones's trip a few months later, in reverse.

Anne Applebaum's groundbreaking work *Red Famine: Stalin's War on Ukraine* was my research bible. Indispensable was the HREC database—Holodomor Research and Education Consortium (holodomor.ca) for its extensive collection of maps, photograph directory, papers, and documents, including survivor accounts and teaching resources.

Why this story matters so much to me

My Ukrainian-born grandfather was a Canadian Communist Party member. Gido (the equivalent of Gramps) had emigrated to Canada just before the First World War but was arrested as an "enemy alien" and interned in Jasper, Alberta. After the war, many people turned their backs on the internees, but the Communists set up soup kitchens.

Gido applied to visit Soviet Ukraine in order to locate his mother and sister, but his application was rejected. When Gido heard about the Holodomor, he shunned everything Stalin stood for, but he kept his friendship with his Canadian Communist friends. When he was buried in the 1960s, his eulogy referred to him as Comrade Forchuk.

For the record: The first federal vote I ever cast was for the Communist Party of Canada, largely due to the influence of my high school geography teacher, who had high praise for Stalin's five-year plans. But for the fluke of time, I could have been Alice.

The Holodomor is still considered a forbidden topic in many parts of the world, and Vladimir Putin, the current Russian dictator, still denies it happened. Those who shed light on the Holodomor are subjected to public abuse.

Before I wrote books, I was a freelance writer for a few local publications. In the late 1980s I wrote a long article on the Holodomor for the local newspaper. After the article was published, I received anonymous phone calls (no caller ID back then) from people threatening to kill me for writing about it. The police sent plainclothes officers to my public events to help ward off trouble, but that wasn't the end of it. Swastikas were spray bombed on a family dwelling, and threatening letters arrived by post. I told my newspaper editor about this, thinking it was newsworthy. Instead, he said my articles were no longer needed. In some ways that was a blessing because it spurred me to write books instead.

When my picture book *Enough*, a Grimm-like fable set during the Holodomor, was published in 2000, the hate started anew. Ditto in 2006 when my short story "The Rings" was published.

The hate has mostly stopped since May 2008, coinciding with Canada's recognition of the Holodomor as an act of genocide against the Ukrainian nation. That same month, I was honored by President Victor Yushchenko of Ukraine for my writings on the Holodomor. He bestowed me with the Order of Princess Olha, the highest award given to foreign citizens.

The House of Representatives of the US Congress recognized the Holodomor as a genocide of the Ukrainian nation in December 2018, and the resolution was adopted unanimously by both houses. More than a dozen countries worldwide have now acknowledged the Holodomor as a genocide.

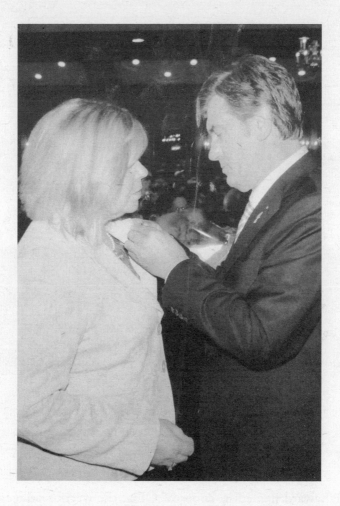

President Victor Yuschenko, right, pins the Order of
Princess Olha on Marsha Skrypuch's lapel on May 28,
2008, at a ceremony in Toronto, Canada.

The Order of Princess Olha is a Ukrainian presidential award named in honor of Olha, the warrior princess and saint of Kyiv. This state award is the highest form of honor given to women for outstanding achievements and distinguished services in educational, cultural, and other spheres of public activity.

• • •

The map on the following pages shows Soviet Ukraine and its borders in 1933. The gray shading reflects which areas were worst and least affected, and illustrates that most of those who starved were from the Ukrainian areas of the Soviet Union.

The map also shows that the area around Kharkiv is one of the worst areas of famine. The tractor plant was on the eastern outskirts of Kharkiv, and I imagined my Felivka to be about ten kilometers away from the plant.

Rate of population decline in the Soviet Union, 1929–1933

- 20% or more
- 15–19.9%
- 0–14.9%

— International boundary
···· Soviet Socialist Republic boundary
■■■ Ukrainian ethnolinguistic boundary

POLAND

Kyiv ◉

Ternopil ◉

Zbruch River

CZECHOSLOVAKIA

HUNGARY

ROMANIA

EUROPE

ATLANTIC OCEAN

Area of detail

BULGARIA

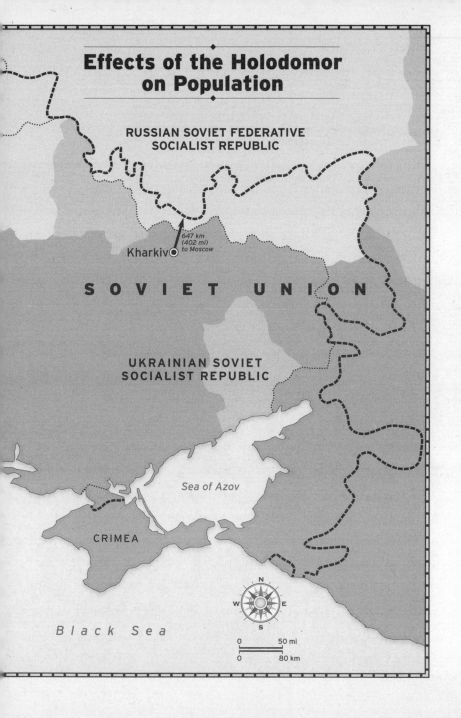

Effects of the Holodomor on Population

RUSSIAN SOVIET FEDERATIVE
SOCIALIST REPUBLIC

647 km
(402 mi)
to Moscow

Kharkiv

S O V I E T   U N I O N

UKRAINIAN SOVIET
SOCIALIST REPUBLIC

Sea of Azov

CRIMEA

Black Sea

N
W   E
S

0   50 mi
0   80 km

ACKNOWLEDGMENTS

I AM EXTREMELY grateful to the people at Scholastic Canada, Scholastic Inc., and Scholastic Book Fairs for enabling me to write my stories and get them into the hands of readers. For this book in particular, a big shout-out to Jana Haussmann of Scholastic Book Fairs for encouraging me to write a middle-grade novel on this topic. Big thanks also to Olivia Valcarce, Diane Kerner, and Sarah Harvey for your faith, support, and extreme patience in helping me tame this particular dragon. Aimee Friedman, thank you for your continued encouragement and support. Dean Cooke, thank you for always being there. And Maral Maclagan, what would my stories do without you?

Thank you, Jars Balan, for your extensive work on the life of Rhea Clyman and for your generosity in sharing your notes with me. I look forward to reading your biography of Rhea when it is published. Thank you, Dr. Matthias Kaltenbrunner, for sharing with me your work on Canadian Ukrainians who migrated to the Soviet Union in the late 1920s and early 1930s. Thank you, Valentina Kuryliw of the Holodomor Research and Education Consortium, for all your help and dedication.

Dad, thanks for letting me bend your ear week after week as this story evolved. Orest, thank you for the tea, the hugs, and the perfect eggs during the many writing marathons.

ABOUT THE AUTHOR

MARSHA FORCHUK SKRYPUCH is a Ukrainian Canadian author acclaimed for her nonfiction and historical fiction, including *Making Bombs for Hitler,* *The War Below*, *Stolen Girl*, *Don't Tell the Nazis*, *Trapped in Hitler's Web*, and *Traitors Among Us*. She was awarded the Order of Princess Olha by the president of Ukraine for her writing. Marsha lives in Brantford, Ontario, and you can visit her online at calla.com.